Zander

Hathaway House, Book 26

Dale Mayer

ZANDER: HATHAWAY HOUSE, BOOK 26
Beverly Dale Mayer
Valley Publishing Ltd.

ISBN-13: 978-1-778860-28-7
Print Edition

Books in This Series:

Aaron, Book 1

Brock, Book 2

Cole, Book 3

Denton, Book 4

Elliot, Book 5

Finn, Book 6

Gregory, Book 7

Heath, Book 8

Iain, Book 9

Jaden, Book 10

Keith, Book 11

Lance, Book 12

Melissa, Book 13

Nash, Book 14

Owen, Book 15

Percy, Book 16

Quinton, Book 17

Ryatt, Book 18

Spencer, Book 19

Timothy, Book 20

Urban, Book 21

Victor, Book 22

Wesley, Book 23

Xavier, Book 24

Yvonne, Book 25
Zander, Book 26

Boxed Sets and Bundles
https://geni.us/Bundlepage

About This Book

Welcome to Hathaway House. Rehab Center. Safe Haven. Second chance at life and love.

Zander finds it hard to believe he's finally made it to Hathaway House—months after Xavier came here. Although his friend is still here to greet him on his arrival, Zander's essentially on his own. Seeing the contrast between Xavier before and now is amazing. His success should be something that springboards Zander to follow in his friend's footsteps, but Zander's frail health is always there in the background, holding him back.

Nelly, a recently hired nutritionist, is thrilled to be at Hathaway House and seeing Zander's weak body reminds her of all the reasons she went into this field. He's desperately in need of every bit of help that the staff here can provide. Just to add to the chaos, a large wedding is being organized for Dani and Aaron.

For Zander, seeing the happy couple reminds him of all that's missing in his life and all that just might be here for him, if he can but reach out for it.

Z ANDER TOLSTON WATCHED out the window of the ambulance—or interfacility transfer or whatever they called this—as it pulled up to a ramp.

When the back doors opened, his attendant smiled at him and announced, "You've arrived."

"Glad to hear it," he muttered, controlling his pain.

He looked at the big building that he'd spent months and months getting accepted into. His military teammate and hospital room partner, Xavier, had already left after his rehab time at Hathaway House, but had promised to come visit. Apparently a wedding was happening a few months from now, but all kinds of plans for it were still ongoing.

Zander just wanted rehab plans for himself. He hoped the wedding wouldn't detract from getting the care he needed here, but he was prepared to trust what everybody had told him—that Hathaway House was the place where he needed to be. He'd wanted to come for so long, and now he was here. It seemed to be a miracle. He looked around as he was helped out of the transport vehicle and into a wheelchair.

Even as he sat down again, the pain jarred him throughout his body. He had survived his injuries, but he had broken his pelvis, both legs, and several ribs. Multiple surgeries had attended to his pelvis and legs. His ribs had been wrapped and took forever to heal. Even now, if he took too deep of a breath, several ribs reminded him that they were still in flux. Plus, his weakened immunity also kept him down. He blew out a huge exhale.

"We'll get you inside and get you settled," the attendant said. "You'll be just fine."

"I hope so," Zander replied, looking around. "Hathaway's way bigger than I thought."

"They did a massive expansion recently," the attendant shared, "which is a good thing, since the demand for this place is insane."

"As long as they keep up the good work," he murmured.

"I haven't heard anything to the contrary. Everybody I know of who's here, or who has been here, loves it."

"That's good to hear. I have a good friend who came through this place, and he's already come and gone. I was hoping to be here … before he left, but he did amazingly well."

"I think a lot of people do amazingly well here," the guy noted, as he wheeled Zander up the ramp. "And I suspect you will too."

Zander looked over, grateful for the vote of confidence. "Maybe. It seems as if I've been a sickly child for a very long time."

"You're not a child now, and, after what you've been through, I don't think anybody'll see you in that light."

"That would be good too," he noted, with a smile, as he looked around. "It's quite the place, isn't it?"

"It is. Now here you go, up and in through the front door."

And, with that, he was pushed into a reception area. A group of people stood around.

One woman detached herself, walked over, and greeted him. "Hey. What's your name?"

"Zander, Zander Tolston."

"And you are the arrival I've been waiting for," she murmured. She reached out a hand to shake his and introduced herself. "Nelly, the nutritionist here. And I understand that we have some immunity to build up with you."

"Yeah, you could say that. I seem to catch everything going around."

"That's okay," she murmured. "We'll get you fixed up just right." At that, she motioned at another woman, calling out to her, "Dani."

This was Dani, the woman who managed the place. Yet she looked way too young for the job title. Her smile that came his way was electric.

"Hi," she said. "Welcome to Hathaway. We do have your room ready, so let's get you in and settled right away."

As Nelly wheeled him to his room, and Dani walked alongside him, he looked around and shared, "Xavier told me a lot about this place."

"That's good to hear," Dani replied. "You should feel right at home. Plus, you'll see him sometime soon, I'm sure. He's no longer a rehab patient, but we see him often."

"He told me about his time here, and I'm really happy for him. He did way better than he expected."

"A lot of people do," she murmured. "And you might find that that'll be the same for you too."

"I hope so. Right about now, I have to admit I'm not feeling 100 percent."

"Nope, nobody is when they first get here," Dani stated, "and the change can be overwhelming very quickly."

He nodded. "I can see that. I'm not sure why, but just a

lot is going on."

"And nothing is important for you to figure out right now," she noted, "except to rest. We'll give you the tools that you need to contact any of us, and Nelly here will get you a nutritional shake full of vitamins and minerals to help bolster your system. We have orders from your doctors to ensure that we do the best we can to add some weight to you and to get your immune system strengthened."

"Yeah, that would be helpful," Zander agreed, "not to mention getting me back on my feet, and with any luck, back to living a normal life."

"We'll do everything we can," Nelly declared in a bright, cheerful voice.

He looked over at her. "Aren't you awfully young? Both of you."

Nelly laughed. "Is twenty-nine *awfully young*?"

He nodded. "It seems sometimes, yes."

"Maybe," she conceded. "And how old are you?"

"Thirty-three," he replied, "and I feel as if I've lost twenty future years of a potential healthy life just because of all the injuries."

"Injuries can totally set you back," she declared. "So we'll have to ensure that the rest of the years you have are at peak performance."

"Oh, I like the sound of that," he muttered, looking at her.

She smiled. "Hey, we're here to help. Follow our instructions, trust us, and give us a chance, and we'll do the best for you that we can."

And, with that, he was pushed into a private room with its own bath. He frowned. "I get a room to myself?"

"You do," Dani confirmed. "And, yes, you're special, but

we do try to give everybody a private room, just like your friend Xavier had one."

"I did hear about that. I just figured he was lucky."

"He was very lucky," Nelly stated, with a smile. "But you're here now, in our hands, and that makes you lucky too."

He looked up, and, for the first time in a long time, he almost believed her. He nodded. "In that case, bring it on."

Chapter 1

Z ANDER STEPPED OUT of the wheelchair with the assistance of Nelly and Dani. Zander wasn't sure those two tiny women could keep him from falling. As soon as his one good foot landed on the floor, he sneezed. Nelly looked at him with a raised eyebrow. He held up a hand. "I'm fine. I'm fine," he muttered, looking around at his new room.

"Are you sure?" Nelly asked.

"Absolutely. I'll be fine." He just wanted to get settled in and to have nobody else look at him with that same look—as if to say, *Hey, bud, you're sick. You shouldn't be here.* That was the last thing he wanted right now for himself. He hated the fact that he'd been big and brawny and had turned into this sickly person he'd never been before. Seems as if he caught everything that came by, with zero resistance to anything. He got the message, loud and clear. His immune system was shot, and he was working toward building it all back up again. He was desperate to not have anything affect his ability to stay here.

With assistance, he slowly made his way into his bed. He stifled his pain as much as he could. He wanted everybody to leave so he could lie down and moan.

Dani smiled at him. "We'll give you some time to adjust to your surroundings. So, unless you need something from me or Nelly right now, we'll come back a little later."

Zander nodded, not saying anything. He watched Nelly follow Dani out of the room. Nelly had long auburn hair tied back in a braid. It swung when she walked.

As the two women headed for the door, a knock came, right before the door opened and an enthusiastic male came bounding in. The two women smiled at him and then waved goodbye to Zander, shutting the door behind them.

It took a moment for Zander to register who it was. Staring at his visitor in shock, he muttered, "Good Lord, Xavier?"

Xavier gave him a beaming smile and walked over and hugged him. "You finally made it," he exclaimed. "I wanted to be here for your arrival, but it just seemed as if everything was pushed back and pushed back."

"I know," Zander muttered, followed by a wry smirk. "All I did was get sick and more sick and even sicker. I didn't think I would ever get here."

"But you're here now." When Zander tried to get up out of bed, Xavier just shook his head. "Sit right there."

"And what good will sitting do?" Zander asked.

"Because you're not ready to dance," Xavier replied. "Start where you can start."

Zander studied Xavier intently. "I can't believe you now," he said in awe. "You're positively glowing. You look … strong, vibrant, healthy, while I feel like an aging invalid." Zander was seriously envious and yet … hopeful. Could he end up as strong as his buddy?

"I am all that and more," Xavier replied. "I have a complete new lease on life. I'm back. My body vibrates with energy. I'm strong," he shared, "and it's all because of Hathaway House. So this is where you need to be too."

"Well, I tried," he teased, with an eye roll at his friend.

"You got my spot."

Xavier smiled. "Everything happens in its own time and place."

Zander groaned. "Where are you getting that gibberish from?"

"Hey, this place is full of that stuff." He smiled. "You have no idea what a culture shock you're in for."

Zander frowned at him. "What do you mean?"

"Your comment about being an invalid? No one's in very good shape when we first arrive, but, by the time we're ready to leave"—he stepped back and motioned at himself—"look at me."

"I am," Zander declared, trying to keep the jealousy out of his tone. "I'm not exactly sure what happened to you, or what you've been taking, but I want some."

His friend burst out laughing. "Then listen to the staff here at Hathaway," he replied. "Listen to them and follow what they tell you to do."

His tone held such an emphatic declaration that Zander frowned. "Sounds like a story is behind that."

"Not really," he noted. "The journey is about trust. Although we have been on multiple journeys that we had seemingly figured out, this one's different." Xavier looked down at his watch and winced. "I'm so glad I managed to see you when you arrived, but I do have to run."

"Of course you do. I'm so sorry that you aren't still staying here."

"That's okay 'cause I'll be back and forth. I'm so happy that I was your first visitor, and I promise I'll be back soon. Not tomorrow though, because you need to just rest and recuperate from the trip here. I'll come by this weekend," he shared. "You've got my cell number. You know I'm here locally, so it's all good."

And, with that, Zander watched as Xavier dashed off. Zander immediately felt a sense of loneliness and even abandonment. Yet that might have more to with Xavier's successful progress than his leaving the room. Zander couldn't believe the energy in Xavier's body or in his spirit.

Then another knock came on his door, and Dani stepped in to ask, "Do you need a pain pill? Don't be shy about speaking up."

Zander shook his head.

She pointed to the Call button on the remote for his bed. "If you change your mind, just press that button. If you have any questions, just ask me or anyone else who is around." She paused, giving him a chance to speak, but Zander remained quiet. "My father and I built this place, specifically to help him. You'll see him around this place."

"Ah." Zander nodded. "I do remember reading something about that on the website."

She smiled and nodded. "And rehab's a journey, a journey with ups and downs, but, through it all, it's forward progress," she shared, "so keep that in mind."

He shifted in his bed and winced.

"I see you're already in pain, and you've got a sweat going on, and we don't want you to overdo it." She sent a quick text.

He winced because obviously they had already seen what he was hoping they wouldn't see, which was his weak system and his frail body. "I'm really hoping that you guys can do something to regain some of my health," he murmured.

"We can," Dani declared. "Nelly, as your nutritionist, specializes in getting everybody's systems back up to optimum health. She and Dennis monitor a lot of the green vitamin drinks you'll soon see, as you'll have at least one a day, if not multiple times a day. Shane is head of our PT rehab program. He's part of your team, and we'll have a rehab plan set up for you soon. Regardless, as time goes on, we'll tweak that plan to make you as good and as strong as you can be."

He frowned. "So the green drinks have vitamins in them?"

Dani nodded. "To a certain extent, yep. Today's will have some pain medication as well. If need be, we'll do some vitamin shots too, depending on what your Hathaway doctors say, after they sort out your medicals."

"You have doctors here?"

"Yes, several are in-house on rotating shifts. Plus, we have specialists in town, depending on what's needed."

"This place is way bigger than I thought," Zander admitted.

"It is quite big. It doesn't hurt that we've just done a rather large addition." She chuckled. "Yet, with all additions come growth and some adjustments to be made."

He wasn't sure if some hidden message was in that, but, hey, he was just glad that he was here. "I'm happy to have a private room. Most places don't have that."

"That was part of why we did our expansion. We don't want people isolated, but we know how important it is at the end of the day to have your own space."

He could appreciate that. He didn't know exactly how tough the rehab days would be, but he knew that Xavier had definitely had a few days that were nothing he wanted to talk about. … Still, that would be Zander's journey ahead. He was just hoping that he could face it without wanting to puke and then pass out. He looked around the room.

Dani handed him an e-tablet and several paper documents. "You need to read over and sign these. And the tablet," she explained, "has your schedule, your team and how to contact them, and quite a bit of information about how the system works here," she explained cheerfully. "I know Xavier's probably told you a lot about it, but that doesn't mean he didn't have some holes in that first-hand experience that he shared with you."

"I guess it's possible. I know he's certainly a huge fan of the work you guys do here."

"Good." Dani nodded. "That's what we like to hear. Your success is our success."

And it sounded trite, but he knew that she meant it. He looked around and noted, "I did have some personal belongings."

"Yep, the paramedics brought them in. I'll have them brought down for you. It is four o'clock, and dinner begins in the next hour," she shared. "If you want a hand to get down there, I will come get you. Otherwise I'll leave it up to Nelly, who'll be here in a few minutes with your first dose of supplements."

He frowned at her and asked, "Like swallowing supplements?"

"Liquids, so the green drinks I mentioned," she clarified. "They're generally easier and faster to absorb."

He nodded slowly. "Maybe, but it might impact my ability to eat too."

"That's what the first few days will be all about," she noted. "We have to know what will work for you and what won't." She motioned at the stack of paperwork in his lap. "Now, on that tablet," she added, "are all our names and contacts of everybody in your team. Each team member will pop in over the next couple days to say hi and to introduce themselves and to get to know you a little bit. So I'll leave you for now because I hear Nelly coming back."

And, with that, Nelly popped in, a bright smile on her face.

Dani stepped out and waved. "If you have any questions, just get a hold of us." And she was gone.

NELLY WATCHED ZANDER study her, as she approached with the big green drink in her hand.

He stared at it and frowned. "That's an awful lot."

"It is," she agreed. "The question is, whether food sits or doesn't sit. We have your file, but that doesn't mean it's been updated."

"Food sits as long as it's not too hard to digest," he stated. "Generally I have a raving appetite, but I'm not exactly gaining weight."

"Right, and we'll work on that. You've got six months here, so it will take however long it takes to get you back on your feet."

"And have you had anybody who couldn't recover, who came in sickly and didn't do well?"

She shook her head. "So far, since I've been here, everybody has done well," she said. "The difference is the time frame that it takes to show the improvements that you want to see."

He stared at her. "And I guess that's one of the challenges, isn't it?" he murmured. "Your time frame versus mine."

"Absolutely." Nelly studied the young man on the bed in front of her. He looked a lot younger, mostly because of the pallor in his skin, and to some extent, the more wasted-away look to his body. Still he would do just fine here. "We have specialists here. We will analyze everything until you're sick of us."

He muttered, "And that's fine, as long as I show signs of improvement. … I don't care what you do, just please help me get my life back."

She nodded. "So let's get some of this down, starting with just half of this, and we'll see how you manage."

He tasted it tentatively and then frowned again. "It tastes good." He looked down at it. "What's in it?"

Such suspicion filled his tone, she had to laugh. "Vitamins, minerals," and she named off a whole pile of other supplements. "Plus, Dani asked that a mild pain medication be included this time too."

He looked at her. "And you don't think this drink will come right back up?"

"I hope not," she replied, pulling up his file on her own e-tablet. "I don't have anything down about you vomiting."

"No, not generally. My stomach wasn't badly damaged in the accident. I eat whatever I want, it seems. Yet I still get sick and can't gain weight."

"That's because your immune system's shot," she murmured. "And that's okay too."

"It is?" He stared at her.

"Let me rephrase that. Your immunity is okay for the moment, but we will get it built up too."

"You really think so?" he asked hopefully.

She smiled at him. "I know so. Give us some time, and we'll get there." She motioned at his glass. "Tip up a bit more."

He looked down at the glass and took a big slug. By now

it was half gone. "It tastes decent. I could get used to this."

She smiled. "Good, because it certainly has a lot of nutrients in there that your body needs. As far as meals, you need to focus heavily on vegetable-rich meals, plus carbs for strength and protein to build muscle."

"So, a balance of all three," he noted, with a smirk.

Chapter 2

NELLY WANTED TO laugh at his reaction to the nutritional supplement drink in his hand. She'd seen many similar expressions on other patients. There seemed to be a universal look of quickly veiled horror when the patients first saw it, but they quickly came to understand its many benefits, especially since it tasted good. In this case, Zander seemed to need this green drink and his three meals a day more than most.

"To a certain extent, yep, your diet is about balance," she murmured. "Ease off the garbage carbs and focus on the good carbs."

He hazarded a guess. "I think you mean that potatoes and yams are okay, but maybe slow down on the pastries and sugar and those things."

"Including juice," she noted. "If you'll fill your system with anything, confirm it's fully packed with nutrition."

He nodded slowly. "Okay. I'm not exactly sure what all that might entail, but I'm willing to try."

She asked, "Did they go over your nutrition, your food choices, and your particular diet back at the other center?"

He stared at her. "What diet?" he quipped. "I ate what everybody else did."

She nodded. "You will eat like everybody else here too," she clarified, "but with a caveat that what is good for you is not necessarily the same for everybody else. So you will *not* follow a special diet, but we will give you the leeway to choose within that diet the foods that you need."

"So I'm not getting a special diet," he replied cautiously.

"No, not at all," she agreed, "but you certainly don't get to have cinnamon buns for breakfast every day. You'll get sausage and eggs, granola, oatmeal, or something along that line."

"Okay, that's fine." He nodded. "Do I get any sweets?"

"You can have a little bit as an afterthought," she shared. "Food first, as dense and heavily nutritious food as possible." She glanced down at her phone. "It is coming up close to dinnertime. I'll be off work here in a few minutes. How about I come back, and I'll take you down for dinner? I'm going that way anyway as it's my dinnertime too. And I'll introduce you to Dennis, who'll be looking out for you and will sort out your first meal."

Zander hesitated. "Sounds good, but will it be complicated?"

"No, not at all," she stated, "I don't see any reason to make this complicated. We just want to confirm that you eat lots of good food."

"Well, I'm hungry. I'm almost always starving."

She nodded. "And that often is a sign that you haven't been getting the exact nutrients that you need for the healing and the muscle-building that you have to do here," she pointed out. "So, in your case, it's even more important that we get you chock-full of as many vegetables as possible."

"And let's not forget the protein," he added. "I'm always craving protein."

"And again we're talking about balance. So, get yourself settled, take a look at your iPad." She brought up the screen on his and showed him where all his team was listed. "Here's your menu for the week. Here's your schedule—which, at the moment, should be pretty open with just testing and resting," she said. "It'll give you a chance to take a look at what you've got coming up. And I'll be back in, say, twenty minutes." And, with that, she turned and left.

FOR THE FIRST time in a very long time, Zander found himself alone. And that's when he realized his bag had already arrived, too. He climbed out of bed and sat in his wheelchair. He rolled his way over to the closet, quickly opened it to see a lot of empty space. He unpacked, moving slowly as he sipped away at his drink, wondering at a place that put nutrition ahead of everything else. It's not as if the other place didn't care. It's just they didn't have the budget, time, or energy to care much.

There were individuals who cared back there too, but there certainly weren't a whole lot of extras in the way of attention. And Zander didn't want to be anybody who needed more attention because there were always those people at the various centers. Ones who were sick, ones who thought they were sick or needed more attention, or were currying favor to get something, including drugs. That was another huge problem in every center. But Zander was here, and Hathaway House seemed to be a completely different story. Man, he wanted to have all the benefits. He was completely geared to getting better.

By the time he had unpacked his bag and had tested out his new bed in a horizontal position, a knock came on his door.

Nelly poked her head around the corner and smiled at him. "Hey. Is the bed comfy?" she teased.

"Maybe," he muttered, as he slowly slid to the ground.

She motioned at the wheelchair. "I don't know whether Dani mentioned it or not, but today and tomorrow you must use your wheelchair for sure, until you're tested." When he glared at the wheelchair, she shrugged. "We want to save your energy for what's important," she murmured. "And what's important is not appearances."

He nodded. "I'll agree with that." He got into the wheelchair and slowly wheeled toward her.

"So now either I can take you down or you can do it yourself."

"I'll do it myself," he replied a little defensively. Yet he was more focused on this very cute redhead with a long braid down her back—and he'd already checked out that she wore no rings. After all, Xavier had found a partner in this crazy place, which was already incredibly amazing. But Zander had to admit that a part of him was hoping somebody would be out there who would take a look at his weak and frail body and not care, instead seeing the warm-hearted soul inside.

As they slowly made their way down the hallway, he muttered, "I don't mean to hold you back."

"Hold me back?" she repeated, frowning at him. "You're not doing that. No point in getting there early, as the people move through the line pretty fast anyway."

"And you get dinner here?"

"Yep, sure do," she confirmed. "I just moved into a residence on-site at one of the housing buildings." He stared at her in surprise. She smiled. "Dani has rehabbed and put in singles' accommodations, and we have a few married couples' accommodations too, so that the staff doesn't have to do as much traveling back and forth."

"Wow," he murmured.

She pointed out things as they headed to the dining room. "I don't know if you can see over there," she began, stopping at a hallway intersection, pointing to some huge windows. "Horse pastures are there. Up here," she added, "we have a big pool table."

He laughed. "I used to play pool. Matter of fact I used to be a heck of a pool shark. But that was a long time ago, when I could put my body into the positions I needed. Right now I would probably fall over."

She smiled and patted his shoulder. "You can always tell Shane about that, and we can work hard on getting you back to normal."

"Not even sure what *normal* is anymore."

"Good, then find a new normal." He frowned at her, but she shrugged and continued. "We get guys coming in here, missing all kinds of body parts," she explained. "They all have the same adjustment period to their new normal. And the sooner you can find a way to live and to adjust to whatever normal is in your life, then you have done well for you and for your family."

"I have a kid sister in university," he shared. "My parents are in England, but I haven't really had too much to do with them. They flew over when I had my accident, saw I would live, and took off again."

"Ouch," she muttered, "doesn't seem they care too much."

"I think having children was something they were expected to do, so they did, but they're scientists and would much rather live in their lab."

She nodded. "Got it," she said, with a smile. "It's not

necessarily a bad thing."

"No, they are dedicated to what they do. I'm dedicated to what I'm doing. My sister is trying to follow in their footsteps, I think. … She's taking science classes, but maybe she's heading into medicine."

"We need more doctors, so good for her in whatever field she ends up in," Nelly shared, with a smile.

They came around a corner, and he saw huge double doors, wide open. And heard a lot of noise. "I gather from the noise that's the kitchen and the dining room."

"Yep," she replied, lifting her nose.

He lifted his and moaned. "Oh, I don't know what that is, but now I'm really hungry."

"I did notice you finished your green drink," she pointed out.

"I did, and it was really good."

"Soon as we see what's up for dinner, we'll sort out what you should have."

"But I get a choice though, right?" he asked, feeling a sense of anxiousness inside him. Something about his love of food and knowing from Xavier just how good the food here was, Zander was afraid he would miss out on some of it.

"Absolutely you choose," she stated. "It's not a case of *You only get to have what you want on Sunday*," she explained. "It's just a matter of making sure we make the best choices, especially here at the start."

As she walked up to the front of the buffet, and they slowly moved through the line, Zander saw people on crutches, people on arm supports, people in wheelchairs, people on prosthetics. Right away he knew he would feel right at home here, and soon. Yet he also noted a lot of able-bodied individuals as the staff and the patients mingled. That was a surprise to him. At the last center it had been all about the residents getting food, and the staff were on the other side of the counter. When Zander and Nelly reached the beginning of the buffet table, he saw a huge man on the other side, flashing a big smile.

Nelly looked over at him and said, "Dennis, this is Zander, our newest resident."

Dennis's eyebrows shot up. "Hey, you're Xavier's friend."

"That I am." Zander grinned. "I don't know what you fed him, but, man, I want some."

At that, a booming laugh filled the cafeteria. Everybody had big smiles on their faces, and something was just so infectious about people so obviously happy with life and their role in it.

Zander looked up at Nelly and asked, "So what do I get to eat?"

She turned to Dennis and stated, "Maximum nutrition at all times for Zander. He's got quite a weak immune system, catches everything flying around, and he definitely needs to build a ton of muscle—but first and foremost we need to give him the ultimate in nutritional support."

Dennis nodded. "Is he the young man I just helped with that green shake?"

She nodded. "Yeah, and we added a lot of amino acids and a couple other things to it."

Dennis nodded. "Good enough." He looked down at Zander and asked, "So, red meat, fish, or chicken?"

"Red meat," Zander replied instantly.

And, with that, Dennis cut him several thick slices of roast beef that had Zander's stomach already gurgling.

"Gravy?" Dennis asked, looking over at Zander.

Zander nodded almost mutely, as he watched as hot gravy was poured over the roast beef.

And then Dennis moved over to the roasted veggies. "Now I would say a ton of roasted veggies for you too." Dennis scooped up a good pile on the side. "Plus some potatoes because you need a bit of carbs. And how about a nice Caesar salad on the side?" He looked over at Zander and added, "You have to tell me when to stop."

"Can I ask you to increase?" Zander replied. "I could use twice those veggies."

With a happy smile Dennis complied, handed over the plate, and then grabbed up a fresh plate and served him a big serving of Caesar salad, grating fresh parmesan on top. He handed that over and asked Nelly, "That suit?"

Nelly nodded. "If he can get that down, it'll be a good start."

"You just watch me," Zander stated. He slowly moved down the line and saw a huge array of desserts and drinks. "Okay, so now I know what you're talking about, and I'm in trouble."

"You eat your dinner first," she replied, "and we'll talk."

He noted that her servings were about half the size of his and her Caesar salad was served in a small bowl, instead of a big dinner plate. He asked, "Aren't you hungry?"

"Sure, but this will do me just fine." Then she laughed. "And remember that I eat here every day."

He nodded as he stared down at the tray of dishes resting on his knees. "A ton of food is here on my lap. Yet a ton more is on offer here. It's pretty amazing. I had visions of typical hospital food."

She laughed. "How about I grab you some water, and then we'll talk about dessert after you're done." She also grabbed cutlery for them and slowly led the way to a table that was mostly empty. Sitting at the end so that he could just pull his wheelchair right up, she helped unload everything on his tray and hers. Then she handed him a knife and fork and said, "Go to town."

He laughed. "You don't have to tell me twice." He cut into the roast beef. He picked up a bite and savored it with closed eyes. "Oh, wow," he muttered, as he went back for several more bites. "I should gain weight on this."

"It's not weight that we need," she clarified in a serene tone. "It's healthy muscle and healed tissue, a chance to regrow and to rebuild. We can't get you back on your feet if we don't have the strong structure in place."

He nodded but wondered at just how absolutely different that mentality was to what he had experienced before. "I was never starved before," he explained, "but I was always left wanting more."

"That'll never happen here," she stated, "but, what you take, you eat."

"Got it." He nodded and spent the next half hour plowing happily through his food.

Dennis stopped by once and brought him a second bottle of cold water, checked that he was eating, nodded approvingly, and took off.

"He cares, doesn't he?" Zander whispered. He was just about done with his beef and veggies plate and spied his Caesar salad. A big fat smile crossed his face. He grabbed his salad and pointed to his empty dinner plate. "Now, I can dig into this."

She laughed. "Most of the guys don't enjoy their vegetables quite so much."

"I'm not *most of the guys*," he declared. "I spent a lot of time where we had no fresh vegetables, and I really like them. Roasted vegetables, skewered vegetables, raw vegetables, I don't care." He shrugged. "Vegetables are good." And he tucked into the Caesar salad with the same aplomb he'd applied to his dinner of roast and veggies. When he was done, he looked over to see that her plate was empty too. He frowned and asked, "Were you waiting for me?"

"Nope, not waiting for anything. Now we'll let that settle and see how your stomach is."

"It hasn't been very touchy," he noted cautiously. "I know I put a lot in it just now." He patted his stomach. "Yet I'm feeling pretty good." He shifted in the wheelchair, trying to ease up his lower back and ribs. "I tend to slouch really badly. It's hard for me to sit up straight for long."

"Got it." She nodded. "How about a coffee and a dessert?"

His face lit up, as he looked back at the big dessert display. "Are you serious? I can have something?"

"Absolutely. What do you want though?"

"That cheesecake," he replied instantly. "The one with all the chocolate across the top."

She chuckled. And almost magically, right at his side, Dennis appeared and put a piece of cheesecake in front of him.

Zander looked up and frowned at him. "How did you know?"

"Are you kidding?" Dennis said, with a smile. "I saw you as you rolled past. I already earmarked a good-size piece for you. Now I'll go grab you a coffee. Just enjoy. And welcome to Hathaway House."

Chapter 3

N ELLY WATCHED ZANDER carefully over the next few days, and he certainly was eating. However, he just wasn't putting on weight. She talked to Shane about it.

Shane nodded. "We see cases like this, where their body's so stressed that it burns through everything that they consume. So, we should see some progress, as soon as he gets a chance to calm down—but it might take a week or two or six," he shared, noting her surprised look. "Remember that the human body can only handle so much at one time, and, if we stress it more than that, he won't do very well. I'm starting his rehab program with very light exercises. He fatigues very easily. So we need to constantly build him up with supplements and green drinks."

She nodded. "I've got down two a day with Zander so far."

"Depending on how well he tolerates it, cut the water volume in half, make them much more intense, and probably give him three if not four a day," Shane suggested.

She nodded. "We can try that starting tomorrow."

"But build him up slowly with that green drink change," Shane added. "Let's keep that stomach solid."

With that, she headed back down to the kitchen to talk with Dennis about it, as he made the shakes, at least the base of them.

He approved of the idea. "We've got several guys on three a day. Let's try Zander with that."

"He's eating plenty though. He is just not yet showing any signs of weight gain."

"It's early days yet," Dennis pointed out. "If we were talking three months down the road with no improvement, that would be a different story."

She nodded. As she turned to leave, Dani walked in, looking harried. Nelly grinned at her. "Isn't getting married fun?"

Dani rolled her eyes. "I still think we should have just got married a long time ago in a very small way."

"Oh, but that wouldn't have been fun for anybody," Dennis protested.

"It's my wedding," Dani declared. "It's supposed to be fun for me too."

He nodded. "And it will be. You just need to get through all this prep work."

"I get it."

And that was the last Nelly heard as she headed down the hallway. She mentally counted off the various patients she worked with. Of all of them, Zander was the only one who was a cause for concern. The others were showing progress, even one who had taken quite a while to show progress was now doing quite well. And she realized Shane was correct. She was the one who was worried. She came up to Zander's door and knocked. A half-hearted reply came from the inside. She pushed open the door, frowning at the odd cry. She stuck her head around and winced.

Zander was half arched and half twisted in bed, not flat and yet not sitting up either.

"Good Lord," she muttered, as she walked forward.

"That looks painful."

"I guess I cramped up, and I didn't realize it," he muttered, gasping. "Until my body froze, and now I can't seem to move."

"I've got Shane on speed dial." And she quickly contacted Shane and told him what was up.

"I'll be there right away," he muttered. "I just finished with another patient."

She looked over at Zander. "He's coming."

"Don't want to bother him," he said, still gasping.

"If you don't think this is bad enough to bother people over, then we have a problem." His grin was more of a grimace, but she accepted it. She walked over and placed a hand on his shoulder. "Does that hurt?"

He shook his head. "No, just everything else."

Then Shane walked in, took one look, and nodded. "Yep, that looks like fun." He turned to Nelly. "You want to send a nurse with a muscle relaxant, please."

"I can do that," she agreed and took off.

SHANE TURNED, LOOKED down at his patient, unscrewed the lid to the jar of homeopathic ointment that he had in his hand, and said, "Let's go."

"Go where?" Zander muttered.

"*Go*, as in, I'll get to work on you." And he gently rolled Zander over, so he was on his stomach and partially off the bed. And then he started to work on Zander's back and side.

Zander laughed, but it came out as a groan. "That feels really good."

"And it'll calm down the muscles pretty fast, once we get

a muscle relaxant down you as well."

With that, Zander tried to relax, but he was always afraid about the pain that came with any movement.

"You'll be fine, just let it go, let the muscles relax," Shane stated, using long smooth strokes.

Finally Zander managed to stretch out a little bit more and to take off yet another layer of pain. "That helps."

Just then a nurse walked in, smiled, and held out the medication. Shane allowed Zander to shift long enough to take it and to get it down. And then he added, "Now lie back down again."

And, with that, Zander stretched out once more to let Shane do his work.

Nelly stood at the doorway and watched. "The muscle massages really make a difference, don't they?" she muttered.

Shane looked over at her and smiled. "Sometimes it's the only thing that does make a difference. Of course the hot tub's good too."

"The hot tub would be great," Zander muttered.

At that, Shane chuckled. "Hey, you're not the only one to think that," he shared. "We do run cycles on it some days. It can get so popular."

"And yet lots of time," she murmured from the door, "it seems to be completely empty."

At that, Shane nodded again. "Not everybody needs it all the time, but it's funny how we do get runs on it. So generally we have people coming and going at a steady pace."

"I would like to be one of the ones going into it," Zander murmured.

"And I would sign you up, but we haven't tested you enough yet to know how you'll get in and out."

"I'll roll in," Zander replied. "How's that?"

"You really want to give it a shot?"

"I sure do," he murmured.

"Fine. Do you think you can sit up?"

And, with his help, Zander sat up, switched his pants out for swim trunks, and together they helped get him into the wheelchair. He flushed as he looked up at her. "Wow, that was a really elegant entrance, wasn't it?"

"Hey, I don't care how it looks," she said, the worry coloring her tone. "I think the hot tub sounds like a great idea."

"Yeah, you coming in with me?" Zander teased.

She laughed. "The fact that I'm off work makes that an interesting invite," she shared. "The fact that you're screaming in pain, not so much."

"I'll be fine," he grumbled, followed by a groan. At that, Shane moved him forward, and he groaned again. "Sitting like this doesn't feel very good."

"Yet most of time you're doing pretty well," Shane noted.

Zander shook his head. "I didn't realize how much that nutritional lack would kick in over this."

"It's hardly just about that," Shane explained. "When you think about it, you've come a long way."

"I guess I have."

"Though everything has to happen in balance," Shane reminded him. "Otherwise we're in danger of causing more trouble than helping."

"If you say so," he muttered, "but the hot tub still sounds good."

"And we're getting there. I promise you that we're getting there." Shane laughed.

They rolled into the elevator that Zander had yet to see and descended one floor. They rolled out and toward the hot tub, when he saw an animal jump in before he got there. Zander asked, "What was that?"

At that, a man came running out from the double doors. "Hey, sorry. That one's mine."

Zander looked down. It was a ferret of some kind—no, a weasel. "Is that an otter or a weasel?" he asked.

"It's an otter. He came in for help, and I lost him out the door. Of course it headed right for the water."

"But why warm water?" Zander asked, staring at it.

The animal rolled over and over, as if having a grand old time.

Nelly laughed. "Stan, I've never seen anything like it."

"Hopefully I can catch him and can take him back inside again," Stan noted, with a sigh. "Just when you think you'll have a good day, everything blows up."

"Oh, I hear you there," Zander muttered, as he shifted from the wheelchair to the ground and slowly scooched closer to the hot tub and the otter.

The otter looked at him and made a weird clackering sound, then came closer to him.

"So, is he dangerous?" Zander asked.

"No, not at all. He's a pet, and he was having some trouble with a back leg, but you wouldn't know it from here."

"I'm having lots of trouble with my legs, so maybe he can teach me a thing or two." As Zander looked down, he smiled at the otter. "Sorry, buddy, but I have to get in there too."

And, with that, Zander slid into the water, along with the otter.

Zander never expected to go swimming with an otter, but, hey, if that's what the day brought, he was more than fine with it. As he watched the silky critter slunk over the edge and headed to the main pool for a longer swim under Stan's watchful eye.

As Zander sank into the water, he shuddered with relief. "That feels so much better." He moaned. "Just the heat helps."

"And that would be the next thing I did in your room," Shane murmured. "Put a hot blanket on your back."

"Maybe when I return to my room," Zander added, shuddering in joy. "I can't believe how good this feels."

"Even if it's just psychological," Shane began, "it'll always be something that makes you feel better."

"And anything that makes me feel better is a bonus, as far as I'm concerned."

"I can't leave you here unattended," Shane explained, "so I'll grab a chair and stay a while."

At that, Zander opened his eyes and stared at him. "I didn't even think of that. You're off work."

"Doesn't matter if I am or not." Shane gave him a smile. "Sometimes work doesn't end just because the clock strikes 4:00 or 5:00 p.m."

"I get it." Zander looked over at Nelly. "You can go home though."

"We both live here," she pointed out. "So nobody feels like leaving you alone on your own right now." When Zander frowned, she frowned right back and then laughed. "Every time you frown at me, I've decided I'll frown right back but twice as long."

"Except you can't possibly do that," he teased, "because you give up too quickly and laugh."

"I'll have to work on that frowning thing then," she decided. "It's impossible to think that somebody could frown better than me."

"Ha," he murmured as he shifted, closing his eyes, enjoying the teasing now that some of his pain had eased. "The best thing for you is to just forget it and to smile all the time. Besides, you have a gorgeous smile." Then came an odd silence. He opened his eyes to see Shane sitting there on the side bench, a grin on his face, and Nelly eyeing him curiously.

"You say that, and yet your eyes were closed," she noted humorously.

"Of course. I've memorized your smile already," he said instantly.

At that, Shane burst out laughing and asked him, "That line works, *huh*?"

"I don't know if it'll work or not," Zander replied. "If I was in the market, I might have tried it," he shared, "but, around this place, the gals are pretty savvy."

"We have to be," Nelly declared. "There's always a lot of men around who are looking to work the angles."

"Is my line working though?" he asked in a joking tone. "Because, if it is, then dang."

"It's not," she scolded but followed it with a laugh.

"Are you sure?" he asked. "It would be nice if it did work."

"Nope, not at all."

At that, they heard the dinner bell.

"No," he cried out in horror. "Don't tell me that I'll miss out on dinner too."

"Oh, we can't have that happening," Nelly stated. "You don't get enough nutrients as it is."

Zander stared at her. "Do you see how much I'm eating?"

"Yep, I also see it going right through you," she replied, "and, chances are, you are not retaining all the benefits."

He shook his head. "I'm fine, and, if Dennis saves me something to eat, I promise I'll eat as soon as I'm out of here. However, the thought of choosing between food or pain relief?" he shared. "I'm sorry, but pain relief will win out every time."

"And so it should," Nelly confirmed. "Now the question is whether we can get you some food down here." She looked over at Shane. "Are there any rules about that?"

He shrugged. "If there were, they went out the window a long time ago," he teased. "We've had several people lately eat in the hot tub."

"Maybe now that Stan has collected the otter, it would be okay." She hopped up and announced, "Let me go talk to Dennis then."

Zander watched as she disappeared and then shifted his gaze to Shane. "Is she doing what I think she's doing?"

"She'll see if you can get a plate down here," he explained. "And I'm pretty sure the answer will be *absolutely*."

"Wow, what kind of a place is this," he muttered, "where that is even allowed?"

"You don't like the idea?" Shane asked, with a wry grin.

"I love the idea," Zander replied instantly. "Anything that literally stops me from having to move is perfect."

"How will you eat if you're stretched out in the water like that?" Shane asked.

"I'll roll over," he said, with a smile.

"I'm glad you've got a sense of humor."

"After everything I've been through, it's hard not to."

"Sometimes you still don't necessarily get the benefit of it," Shane noted. "But here, you need to just relax and to let some of that stress go away. Was there anything that set this off?"

"I don't think so—at least I wasn't aware of anything."

Shane suggested, "Well, next time you end up like this, can you spend a few minutes thinking about what might have happened just prior to the attack and see if there's a movement, a thought, a stomach gurgle, anything, that's triggering this?"

"Could it be something so simple?"

"Not usually, but there's really no research in a lot of this. Thus we have a unique opportunity here to understand and to learn more. And anything that helps one person learn and improve is something we want to hear about for the next person."

"I get that." Zander let out a deep sigh.

"That came from a long way down," Shane pointed out. "What was that all about?"

"I think that was the last of the pain finally releasing," Zander shared, shifting so that he was sitting upright in the hot tub. Then he scooched backward, so he was sitting on one of the steps under the water. "I have to admit, even if it does feel better, I don't want to leave just yet."

"No need for you to leave," Shane added.

Yet Zander frowned as Shane checked his watch. "You've got a place to go, don't you?"

Shane flashed him a grin. "I have a partner. Sometimes it works to meet up, and sometimes it doesn't."

"Well, if Nelly's returning with food, can she just sit here with me?" he asked, frowning.

Shane frowned right back at that.

"Ooh, I see what she means about that instant frown," Zander said. "It's quite a technique."

At that, Shane burst into laughter again. "You're fast," he replied, admiration in his tone. "Not everybody would be quite so quick on the repartee."

"Hey, I am trying," Zander shared. "And you're not answering my question. Instead you're trying to divert my attention."

"I'm thinking about it, but she's not a trained nurse."

"But she's not an idiot," he declared, raising an eyebrow. "Surely if there's a problem, she can call for help."

"Considering where you're at, it's possible to have a real problem."

He frowned yet again, and, hearing footsteps, he looked up to see Nelly walking down the stairs, with Dani at her side. Zander frowned at Nelly, and she frowned back. He groaned. "That'll get old quickly."

"It does get old quickly," she agreed, "so knock off the frowning."

"Yeah, but you finagled the boss to bring down my food," Zander noted. "That's hardly fair."

"Oh, so I was supposed to get the staff to do this?" Dani asked, with a wide-eyed, innocent look. He frowned again, yet she burst out laughing.

"Right? See?" Nelly pointed out. "He frowns all the time. It's an instinctive reaction to something he doesn't want to hear."

"I think that goes for everybody," Zander protested. "Besides, Shane has to leave, and I was asking him—so maybe, Dani, you can help. Is it okay if I stay in the hot tub, as long as Nelly has a moment or two to stay with me?"

"And I've definitely got a moment or two," Nelly admitted. "I brought down dinner for both of us."

He looked at her in surprise and then grinned. "Even

better." He looked over at Dani. "Can we stay, please?" He knew he sounded like a petulant little boy, yet he wasn't sure if that tack would work or not.

Dani laughed. "Yeah, I can pretty well depend on Nelly here to have a solid head on her shoulders." At that, she looked over at Shane. "Are you okay with it?"

Shane nodded. "I am." And he turned to Nelly. "If he has any trouble getting into the wheelchair on his own, do *not* try to lift him."

"Agreed," she conceded instantly. "I promise I'll call for help."

"I plan to make it into the wheelchair on my own," Zander protested.

"Good plan," she noted, "but just in case that plan doesn't work out so well …"

"*Fine*," he said grudgingly. "I guess that makes sense."

"It does, indeed, so stop your frowning," she quipped. "You got your permission. … Now, how do you want to eat this?"

He looked around and replied, "If you move that tray a little bit closer to the water's edge, I can probably just sit here and eat." And, with that, he sat on the bench sideways and, using just a fork and holding his plate steady, he managed to scoop up food. "I don't even know what this is," he shared, staring at a salad that was green but had something white in it.

"It's a couscous salad. Along with spaghetti and meatballs." Then she added, "I got you extra meatballs."

He grinned at that. "Perfect. And I do like the carbs here too. They're great." And then he realized that it was just the two of them now. She sat down beside the hot tub and rearranged her tray so that she could eat close to him.

"Sorry you're on babysitting duty," he apologized. "I just realized that Shane had a place to go and someone to be with, and I felt bad. But what I didn't consider was that you might have a place to go and somebody to be with too."

"I don't," she stated, with a cheerful smile. "So just eat your dinner and relax."

And that's what he did. He picked up a big meatball and bit into it. "Yum." He closed his eyes. "Okay, something is truly special about the food here."

She murmured, "I know."

He opened his eyes to see her staring at him, a smile playing at the corner of her lips, and then she bit into a meatball herself. "Our chef is one of the hidden secrets about this place," she murmured. "And, if everybody knew, we would have a constant influx of new staff as they tried to get on board. At least coming to see how it all worked."

"Hey, even the visitors would be eating this all up," he muttered. He slowly ate, enjoying every bite. When he was finally full, he put down his fork and stared at the last meatball. "I don't think I can get it down," he admitted.

And such a sadness filled his tone that she burst out laughing. "You may want to just leave it there and wait for a little bit. I bet you can eat that in another five or ten minutes."

"Oh, that's a good idea," he agreed. "I think you're probably right."

"I suggest you stretch out and get that back moving again. You've been sitting in the same position, and I don't want more muscle cramps to return."

Obediently he stretched out full length in the hot tub and noted, "I had no idea hot tubs even came this big."

"For a healing center like this," she added, "it makes sense though."

"Oh, I agree, and I think it's a wonderful idea. I just don't know why everybody isn't in here. And, if they all knew that they can come down here and have dinner in the hot tub, why isn't it full all the time?"

"Because it's not something that appeals to everybody. For some people, it's associated with therapy, and that's not something that they want to deal with all the time."

With his eyes closed, he contemplated her words. "I guess that's a good point. I've barely even begun my rehab."

"True, and this painful cramping muscle isn't a great start," she pointed out. "The good news is, at least we know where some of the weaknesses are, and we can move on from there."

Chapter 4

N ELLY KEPT AN eye on Zander over the next few days, but he did quite a bit better after that one ugly event with muscle cramps. As the days turned into weeks, she was thrilled to see him start to put on a little bit of weight. She mentioned it one day at lunchtime, as she brought over a tray and took note of the serving sizes on his plates in front of him. But he'd been good with his food choices and had packed his plate full of vegetables. Of course, some of it was Dennis's special Greek salad, and she'd packed her plate full of that too. "By Jove, I think you're putting on some weight."

He nodded, giving her a beaming smile. "I think you're right. I haven't been on the scale, so I was going to ask Shane about it."

"I'm sure he would be more than happy to put you on the scale," she replied, "but I can already see that you're filling out a little bit in the face and in the shoulders."

"I'm glad," he said. "It seems as if I got nowhere very quickly at the last place."

"Exactly, and then all of a sudden you got somewhere. And that somewhere, I think, is starting to show. You've been here what now? Almost a month?"

He nodded. "Coming on a month, yes. Progress has been slow," he admitted. "A couple times I wasn't sure I was getting anywhere, but, hey, it looks as if we're slowly pulling in a little bit of success here."

"A little bit is a good start," Shane declared from behind them, as he stood there, smiling down at Zander. "You definitely have put on some weight. We'll do a full workup on your weight and measurements when we get into the gym next time," he shared. "In the meantime, eat your veggies." And, with that comment, he headed on past them to join a group of other therapists, who Zander vaguely recognized.

"He runs a big team here, doesn't he?"

"He does," Nelly murmured. She moved her salad closer and started to dig in.

He smiled at that. "I really like how people here appreciate the food, and nobody wastes it, and they all seem to really appreciate Dennis."

"Dennis and the team behind him," she murmured. "Ilse runs the kitchen. Dennis, … well, he runs the front."

"I get it. I have to admit that Xavier told me a lot about him."

"Good, I'm glad. Anything that gives you an insider's knowledge when you first get here is helpful," she noted. "It makes your initial adjustment to Hathaway House a little bit easier."

"I finally made that adjustment," Zander declared, "and I've seen Xavier a couple times. He looks so fine that it's hard to believe that I might get the same results."

"No reason why you shouldn't, is there?"

"I don't think so, but I'm always afraid that something's wrong with me or something's wrong with the system, and I'll be the one case who never quite gets the same progress."

She burst out laughing, and then she nodded. "I've heard that a couple times, and I understand it. I think I probably felt exactly the same thing in my various training courses. It seems as if everyone else gets it, yet you don't, and you're afraid that you'll be the one person who's either too stupid or too dense, to understand what's going on. Then all of a sudden that light bulb comes on, and you're like, *Okay, now I understand.* And for you here with rehab, it's as if you will be the one person who doesn't see the same progress, the one person everybody else will look at sideways and ask, *What's wrong with him?*"

"Exactly," he cried out.

She poked her fork in his direction. "And that won't happen. You do know that, right?"

He smiled and tilted his head at her fork. "Don't point that thing at me," he teased. "It's got a sharp end on it."

"Actually it has multiple sharp ends," she clarified, with a mischievous smile. "And, if I want to point it at you, I will. So, what will you do about it?"

"I'm not sure," he admitted, fascinated, as he stared at her.

She shook her head. "What's that look for?"

"You're just such fun to be around," he said. "I didn't think rehab could be fun. I didn't think therapy could be fun, and honestly, Shane's not a whole lot of fun."

At that, she burst out laughing to the point that she couldn't stop.

He leaned in and whispered, "Don't let him know that."

She shook her head but continued to giggle.

Finally Dennis walked over and asked, "Are you all right?" And he handed her a glass of water.

She took the water gratefully and nodded. "I am," she murmured. "Zander's got such a great sense of humor."

"*Uh-huh.*" Dennis just looked over at some of their empty plates and pointed. "And a good appetite. I appreciate that." And, with that, he gathered their wiped-clean plates and disappeared again.

She stopped giggling finally and looked over at Zander, wiping the tears from her eyes. "Wow, I can see that you're the one who's fun to be around. I feel like such an old stick-in-the-mud for not having the same sense of humor."

He shrugged. "And so you should. I'm the injured party here," he quipped. "You guys should all be entertaining me."

"Nope," she replied, with a headshake, "but you're doing a great job entertaining me."

"Hey, that's supposed to be a two-way street."

And, with the same amount of fun, they finished dinner. As he looked back at the dessert table, he added, "I didn't quite grab enough, so maybe I could fit in a little bit of dessert."

"I'm going to have an apple pie."

"An apple pie? All to yourself?"

She pointed over her shoulder. "You didn't see them over there, did you? Hang on a minute. Let me go take a look." She got up and headed to the dessert counter. When she came back again, she was holding two whole pies, but they were only about six inches across.

He stared in fascination. "Individual pies?"

"Yeah, and wait until you see what's coming now," she shared, with a smile.

As Zander looked up, Dennis came walking around, a scooper in one hand and a bucket of ice cream in the other.

Zander immediately put up his hand and waved. "Me, me, me."

Dennis, a big grin on his face, walked over. "Look at you guys. Won't be any food left in the house."

"Good," Zander declared, patting his tummy. "Food should be eaten, especially really *good* food."

"Oh, I agree with you, and, whatever you eat, I don't have to put away," Dennis pointed out, as he dumped a big scoop of ice cream on Zander's plate. Then Dennis turned to Nelly.

"Yeah, but one-third of that size," she said, with a head-shake. "I only want to take what I can eat, and, man, I won't eat *that* much."

"That's okay. I'll finish yours too," Zander vowed, with a fat grin.

She stared at him. "Seriously?"

"Yep, seriously," he said.

Dennis was long gone by the time she finished what she could, which sadly wasn't the whole pie. She stared down at it. "This is one of those times when I want to take that sucker home to my place."

"Can't you?" he asked, with an odd expression. "If you live on the place, can't you just take it back to your room and eat it in a couple hours?"

"Well, I could," she conceded. Then she smiled and patted her tummy and added, "Yet absolutely no way I'll eat more in another three or four hours."

"That's too bad," he muttered, with mock sympathy.

She stared at him. "Are you serious? You can eat this too?" He nodded. She steered it a little bit closer to him.

He snatched it and polished off the rest of it in a bite or two. He sat back with a happy sigh. "I don't know how you could possibly *not* have finished it. You were down to just a bite."

"It was a lot more than a bite," she argued, with an eye roll. "But, hey, at least you got to enjoy it."

"That and so much else," he agreed. "What I don't enjoy are the workouts. I don't enjoy always feeling as if I'm behind schedule, and I really don't enjoy that sense of craziness going on around me," he noted. "There seems to be constant conversations, as if people are talking behind my back."

She stared at him and then shook her head. "Not behind your back at all. It's all about the wedding."

"Oh, right. I forgot about that. That's going on, isn't it?"

"It is, and it's in a little over four months, but plans are being made now."

"*Ooo-kay*, got it. Good. I was starting to get a complex. It seemed I would approach, and all of a sudden conversations completely stopped."

She nodded. "It's all about the wedding."

"Well, I'm really happy for Dani. She seems to be a really nice lady."

"And she built this all on her own with her father in mind," Nelly shared. "Her dad came back from a war zone in rough shape."

"Yeah, I heard some about that," he muttered, looking around. "It's pretty fascinating."

"It is," Nelly agreed. "And, just like downstairs, we have her horses and the veterinarian clinic, she also takes in rescues of the canine or of the equine variety—or a rabbit or a llama or whatever," she murmured. "And thankfully her new partner is Aaron, who was one of the first patients who came to the center. They fell in love, and he's completing his vet training, so he'll be working downstairs soon."

Zander stared at her. "Where that otter came from, right?"

She nodded. "Did you get a tour down there?"

"I found myself down there, but I wasn't exactly sure what that place was. I had heard about it a lot from Xavier. I just haven't gone down to see it for myself yet."

"You should. An awful lot is down there that you don't even think about."

"As long as it's good stuff," he replied, "as I can't stand to see an animal in pain."

She nodded in commiseration. "I agree with that. I can't either. But, if you want, I can take you down tomorrow, and we can take a look at the end of our day."

"And do what?" he asked. "What exactly are we looking at?"

"Stan often has animals that you can hug and hold, animals that are recovering from surgery or are alone, animals that have been dumped off and are lost, and they all need cuddles too."

"Done," he declared. "Four o'clock?"

She looked at him in surprise and then chuckled. "Absolutely. Four o'clock. It's a date."

FUNNY, BUT WHEN four o'clock came around the next day, Nelly jumped up from her desk and basically raced out, almost catching Dani by surprise as she stepped in. "Sorry," Nelly muttered.

"Apparently you have places to go and people to see," she quipped, with a smile.

"I do, indeed." Nelly laughed. "Hate to say it, but it's something that I've been thinking of for a while."

"You go then." Dani sent her off with a wave.

As Nelly raced down the hallway to the elevator, she

caught it just at the perfect time, and she was quickly transported down to Stan's. As the elevator door opened, Zander sat there, waiting for her. She laughed. "I was trying so hard not to be late."

"Hey, I don't think you're late at all," he said, with a smile. "Matter of fact, I think you're doing just fine."

"You think so?" she asked in a teasing tone. "And who knew that you would beat me here?"

"I finished a little bit early," he admitted, with a smile. He motioned toward Stan's area. "Shall we?"

"Yep, we sure should." She stepped up behind him and pushed his wheelchair forward.

"Hey, I can do that."

"I'm sure you can," she replied, "but anytime I can take a load off, I will."

"I'm not that sickly."

"And you're not that healthy yet either," she argued.

He grumbled, "Okay, fine. I won't argue that one."

She chuckled. "You know I'm right."

"Sure, but that doesn't mean I want to feel that way."

"Ooh, good point. I'm not trying to make you feel bad."

"Good," he said, now laughing. "And I'll never feel bad when you are honest with me. You're just too funny."

"Hey, I'm quite thrilled with how my day is going. I got through it without any major calamities, got lots of phone calls done, got lots of answers I needed. It's been good."

"That sounds great. Now if only the rest of the day goes so well."

"Are you expecting it not to?"

"Oh I don't know. Life's a funny thing."

"It is, indeed," she agreed.

As they stepped into the vet's office, Robin looked up

and smiled. "Hey, look at that. You want to visit with that otter again?"

Zander beamed. "Is he still here?"

"Nope, sorry, he's gone home."

"Oh, don't tease me like that then," he said sadly, "but I would love to have another animal in my arms."

"We might manage that." Robin stood and quickly came back with two baskets.

He looked inside one, and his heart melted. Five tiny kittens were inside, their tiny faces all curled in together.

"They're beautiful," Nelly exclaimed.

Zander had been given the other basket, filled with something else. She leaned over and studied them. "Are those foxes?"

At that, Robin laughed. "They indeed are. Somebody found them with no mom, so we're doing our best to keep them alive." She pointed behind her. "I'll be back out with feeding bottles in a minute." She returned quickly with several bottles, handed Zander one, picked up one of the baby kits and handed it to him, tucking it up against his chest and explained, "Feed it this way."

"Oh my," he muttered, his face completely enthralled.

Nelly looked up at Robin and winked. "This is such a great place to come visit," she murmured. "Thanks."

"We try hard." Robin nodded. "It's unpleasant to see the animals having a bad time like this, but sometimes we just need the extra help too."

"Any time you want help, just ask me," Nelly offered.

"I know. I know," Robin murmured. "But, hey, you don't always have the time to help either."

"Right," she agreed. "And we didn't give you any notice that we were coming."

"Better you come and don't worry about the notice," Robin replied, smiling. "Absolutely better to come just because."

And, with that, everybody proceeded to feed the babies. The basket of kittens on Nelly's lap didn't stop her from having a baby fox in her arms and a bottle as she nursed it gently. "They are so adorable," she whispered. She stroked the soft fur, watching as the mouth and throat worked actively to take in whatever formula was in the bottle. "Does this happen often?" she asked Robin, who was helping with the feeding as well.

"Not often, no. Yet you can never tell from day to day who might come into the center needing help," she pointed out. "These guys are definitely in need right now."

Just watching the look on Zander's face, Nelly could feel the magic in his heart. But then she didn't need any help with that either, as her own heart was rumbling along quite nicely. When the last little one was full, she looked up to see if another one needed to be fed but found the final one being picked up by Robin. "Now, what will you do with them?" she asked Robin curiously.

"We'll take them back to their cages and let them digest this, which means usually they fall right asleep. They're pretty young yet, so at the moment we're safe from having them trying to run all over the place," she added, laughing.

"Do you have a large-enough cage for when they get bigger?" Zander asked.

"We'll have to start separating them soon. We're looking for a rescue that can take them or somebody who can rehabilitate them back into the wild."

"They are so beautiful," she whispered.

"I agree," Robin muttered, a soft smile on her face. "This

part is when you really enjoy working here."

"I guess there's a lot of days when you don't, *huh*?" Zander asked.

"Only the days that I have to put animals to sleep," she admitted. "Those are always the days that break my heart, each and every time."

At that, Zander winced. "I don't think I could do your job, just because of that."

"And some days I don't think I can either," Robin admitted. "If the animal's old and injured, and it's a kindness, then it makes it easier, but it's still not easy."

"Right," he replied, with a nod. "None of that kind of work would be, I imagine."

"Nope. But it's valuable, and that's something that we have to hang on to," she shared, with a smile. "Just like your rehab job here is to get better, to do the best you can, and to move forward in life, with all this pushing you into your future," she explained. "And that's your job, and nobody else can do that right now for you, and that's important too."

He laughed. "Everybody here is so positive and always looking on the bright side."

"That's because we see so many stories like I do here in this office that aren't so bright and cheerful, for both the humans and the animals," she noted. "Just because you see the brightness around you doesn't mean it's always that way. So we try to hang on to the days and the times when it is."

"I never think about the ones who don't do well here," he noted sadly. "I guess that happens too."

"For more reasons than you can even think about," Robin said. "I've been here a long time, and I've seen people we thought would do phenomenally well, yet come down with some major illness that took them out, and we just didn't have a clue what was even going on inside their system. We've had people go back to hospitals for more surgeries and people who had to go into a hospital because a CAT scan showed things that weren't part of anything we can do to help them," she murmured. "And it's hard, and it's difficult, but it's still worth doing. Anything that heals or reduces the pain is worth doing," she reiterated. Robin took the fox from Zander's arms and said, "Now, you should go have your own dinner." She gave him a bright smile.

"And what about your dinner?" he asked.

"Oh, I'll get mine too," she stated, "but my partner's coming, so we'll be up later."

And, with that, Zander nodded. Everybody seemed to have partners. Everybody seemed to have relationships here, and it really surprised him. After seeing Xavier find a partner for himself here too, Zander felt the same opportunity wasn't necessarily available for him. Look at how well Xavier had done with rehab. He was healed and healthy. As Zander slowly wheeled his way out of the veterinarian clinic, he felt a sadness pulling on him.

"I took you in there to make you happy," Nelly murmured. "I wasn't thinking you would come out sad."

"Sad? Not necessarily. It was just something Robin mentioned about her partner and then seeing all the wedding preparations and all the laughter, and I don't know how much of that is a normal and an everyday occurrence here," he murmured. "But it's such an odd thing to realize that so many people here have relationships."

"And you don't?" she asked.

"No, I don't," he said, with a smile in her direction. "Never thought in many, many years that it would be a thing for me."

"And why wouldn't it be a thing for you?" she asked curiously.

"Only because you never really understand that other people are probably doing better than you. You're the one sitting here and judging the world because they won't like you in your current physical condition," he shared. "When really it's you judging them first, before they get a chance to even see you."

"Ah." Nelly nodded. "We've seen so many relationships happen here that it's not even something that I question anymore. Yet I guess for everybody new who comes in, it's always an intriguing issue, isn't it?"

"I would imagine so, unless they already have someone waiting for them, who is so happy to take them, to know that they survived whatever trauma they went through, and that the condition doesn't even bother them."

"I'm sure that, in some cases, it does bother people. I'm sure there have been a few instances where it's been a less-than-happy outcome, and divorces have happened over it," Nelly noted. "However, I would prefer to think that, in most cases, that's not the norm."

He frowned at her.

"And there's your frown and your worry again," she said, tapping his shoulder lightly. "You focus on you. You get yourself healthy. I'm pretty darn sure the rest of it'll just fall into place."

"Do you think so?" he asked.

"I do," she declared, staring at him. "Seriously I do."

He smiled. "You're a nice person."

"Why? Because I believe in romance, and I believe in love, and I believe in happy-ever-after?" she asked, with a chuckle. "No, I don't think that I'm a nice person just for that. I just want to believe in the goodness of people, even though we see so much of the other side of it," she murmured. "We each get to choose what we look at. We choose how to react to things, and I choose to react positively. ... On that note, we just fed the babies in the clinic, but what about us?"

"I think it's dinnertime," Zander proclaimed, "if you're up for it."

"I'm up for it," she replied. "What about you?"

He nodded. "Absolutely."

And they turned and headed toward the dining room.

WHAT ZANDER DIDN'T know for sure was if he was up for finding out that the only reason Nelly spent as much time with him was because it was her job. He knew that there was that aspect to it, but he didn't want to have it in his face that she was really just being nice because she got paid to do this. And yet he didn't know how to ask her that. Or even if it was something he should ask. How do you ask somebody about that behavior? What right did he have to ask about her motivation?

Feeling a little bit confused and definitely on the downside of a mood, he pulled into the buffet line and asked, "Any idea what's for dinner?"

"The menu is up there," she said, pointing, "but I can't read it yet, not with all these people in line."

He nodded. "I'll check it out when I get up there."

"Nonsense, let me go read it." She walked away and then came back again.

He asked her, "So you couldn't read it from here?"

"I don't have my glasses on," she said, with a sigh.

"Why don't you have your glasses on?" When she flushed, he raised an eyebrow. "Oh, there's a story behind that."

"Yeah, but one you'll laugh at," she said.

"No, not necessarily. Besides, maybe it'll make you seem more human instead of so perfect."

She just stared and shook her head. "Now I definitely don't want to tell you."

"Why?" he teased. "I promise I won't laugh."

"It's still stupid," she admitted. "It's one of those little things that I have hung on to since childhood."

"Oh." He stopped and nodded, now understanding better. "You don't want anybody to see you wearing glasses. Kids can be cruel at times."

"It's not that I don't want anybody to see me in them," she protested. "Lots of people have seen me in my glasses, as I wear them at work all the time. It's just, well, I tend to leave them off when I'm not at work. So that I don't get bugged about it—which is ridiculous because nobody here would do that."

That made him smile in a way because it meant she wasn't *at work* right now with him. "But wearing glasses isn't just about work because you want to see all the time, right? ... Does anybody here really bug you about it?" he asked.

"No, that's why I thought you would be quite surprised at me for even thinking this. It happened in childhood, yet," she admitted, with a shrug, "obviously it still seems to be in my face, even after all these years."

"I can see how, when you were younger it would be harmful being called four-eyes or whatever insults that they used back then. Those remarks were hurtful, made you feel different, but kids can be that way. Sometimes I think we live through that so we grow tougher, bigger, harder skins."

She burst out laughing. "And yet I didn't grow one of those at all."

"And that's because you're hiding your glasses," he teased, with a smile.

"Maybe I'll try to wear them a little more often."

"It would be good for you to see at all times," he reminded her, with a smile. As they sat down he added, "You can spend time with other people too, you know?"

"Of course I know," she agreed, facing him. "I spend time with a lot of people here. It's unavoidable in a way," she muttered, rolling her eyes. "Yet I'm happy to be here right now."

"You sure?" he asked. "I don't want this to be like a work thing, where you feel as if you have to be here with me, when you have friends sitting off to the side."

She chuckled. "Those are the friends I work with," she explained. "Not exactly who I want to spend every moment of my time with. No, I'm perfectly content right here, right now," she murmured. "So sit down and eat."

He looked at her and quipped, "I am sitting."

She rolled her eyes. "*Fine*. I'll eat then."

"Good," he murmured as he watched.

Finally she looked up and asked, "Okay, am I eating weird? Is something wrong?"

He just shook his head and smiled. "You're just really pretty." Immediately a flush washed up her cheeks. He chuckled. "And obviously you aren't used to getting compliments."

"Definitely not used to *that* compliment," she said,

brushing her hair back. "You really surprised me."

"You surprised me," he stated. "I just looked up, and I just … I just saw that, and I wanted to say something."

"Well, thank you," she whispered.

He decided to drop it because it was obviously making her uncomfortable. As they continued eating, he asked, "What do you do in your evenings?"

"Lots of things. Watching TV, scrolling the internet. I do a lot of embroidery, something that's mostly gone out of fashion now," she noted. "I use the swimming pool. I read. I do a bunch of stuff. Sometimes I just sit outside under the stars, although there won't be any stars for a while given the forecast."

"I imagine the evenings in wintertime are beautiful here."

"Not that we get winter per se," she noted, with a nod. "At least not compared to other parts of the country, but it can be truly beautiful."

"I imagine," he murmured.

By the time they finished dinner, she looked as if she was ready to go. So he announced, "I'll head back to my room now. Thanks for a wonderful afternoon."

She chuckled. "We can do it again sometime," she offered.

"I would like that." With a smile, he slowly turned and headed out of the dining room.

As he passed Shane, Shane whispered, "Nice job."

"Nice job on what?" Zander asked.

"She's still sitting there, staring at you," he explained. "Don't look now, but she's obviously interested."

"Oh, I don't know about that. I probably just flummoxed her," Zander said, with a laugh. "She's not sure what to make of me."

"That's probably a good thing right about now," Shane replied thoughtfully. "Yet I can tell she likes you."

"Yeah?" Zander asked. "Well, that's good 'cause I really like her too. She comes from the heart."

"Now that," Shane said, with a bright smile, "is very true. Not only that, she's all heart. We've seen her get quite emotionally attached to various patients who have not necessarily done all that great. It's been pretty hard on her."

"In that case, I'll have to ensure I'm not one of those who doesn't do very well," he declared. "I'll have to be somebody who does great, so she doesn't get upset."

Shane burst out laughing. "If that's what it takes, I am all for it. I don't care what you have to do, but find the motivation to make this the best six months of your life." And, with that, Shane turned back to the tableful of people he was visiting with.

Zander continued to roll out of the dining room and back to his room.

Chapter 5

T HE NEXT FEW days were busy, and Nelly had a trip planned for the weekend. When she came back home late Sunday night, she did her laundry to get ready for work the next day. When she showed up Monday morning, she checked over the weekend's assessments to see what was going on and what lab tests came back for various patients. When she got to Zander's file, she opened it to see what he had experienced over the weekend. As she read through the notes, he was doing fine, except that he hadn't eaten as much. She frowned at that. He'd obviously been eating just fine before she left, so what had changed? Deciding to find out, she got up and walked down the hallway. At his door, she knocked.

When he called out, she opened it, stuck her head around, and greeted him. "Hey, stranger."

"Oh, there you are. I wondered what happened to you."

"I was gone for the weekend," she shared. "If I stay here all the time, then I tend to end up working all weekend."

"Right." He gave her a clipped nod. "I never thought about that. I tend to forget that, just because I'm here seven days a week, and this is my life, it's not your life, is it?"

"Not always," she admitted. "We certainly spend an awful lot of our time here, more than our quoted *salary time* anyway," she clarified, with a smile. "Lots of times it's fine, but sometimes it's nice just to get away."

"Where did you get away to?" he asked curiously. "I hope it was wildly exciting."

"Well, while not *wildly exciting*, it was fun," she conceded. "I saw a longtime girlfriend, who came to visit a mutual friend in town. So I stayed in town with them."

"Nice," he replied. "And I suppose you went out and lit up the town all night long, did you?"

"Oh yeah, right," she quipped. "We went bowling, had dinner out, and then the next day went for brunch, lots of walks outside, some small hikes, generally just had a good time," she shared. "But I see in my notes here that you didn't do very well eating over the weekend."

He looked down at the folder in her hand and frowned. "Those dratted notes. You should just forget about them."

"Well, if you had eaten well all weekend," she replied, "I could, but you didn't eat all that well, so I can't."

He groaned. "It's fine."

"It's not fine," she declared. "Is something going on?"

"Yeah, one of those dark shakes of Dennis's got a little bit too-too rich and, and, as soon as it went down, it came back up. When that happened, everything else in my system decided to revolt," he shared. "So I've just stayed with water and avoided the shakes all weekend."

"Interesting," she murmured.

"That's not quite the word Shane used for it, when he was called in to look after me. And I didn't want him to be called in at all," he stated, raising his hands. "It was stupid. I just guzzled it back too fast, that's all."

"Right, but more than that, how are you feeling now?"

"I'm fine," he stated instantly. "Honest, I'm fine."

She frowned, thought about it, and asked, "You would

tell me if you weren't feeling well though, wouldn't you?"

"Sure," he said carelessly.

But the tone in his voice made her wonder if something was really upsetting him. "I feel as if you're upset with me," she shared.

"No, not at all. You're fully entitled to live your life as you want to."

And then it hit her. "You didn't know I was going away for the weekend, did you?"

He looked at her and shook his head. "No, but then it's not up to you to tell me that, is it?" he asked.

She winced. "I should have told you myself. I didn't even think about it."

"Of course not," he said. "Why would you? Why would you have anything to do with any of us here in this place?" he asked. "We all will leave anyway."

"I hope you do," she stated. "I hope you get well and have a wonderful life after this," she murmured. "But that still doesn't mean that having a little bit of advance knowledge about somebody's plans isn't helpful."

"And yet it really doesn't change anything though, does it?" he asked. "I guess for a while there I was just jealous. You can get up and leave, go away for a weekend, which sounds like Nirvana to me," he admitted. "I was just stuck in a wheelchair. Not exactly sure I'll get out of it anytime soon either."

Not at all sure where all this maudlin talk was coming from, she avoided putting down a note in his file. "Have you had breakfast yet?"

He shook his head. "Probably won't either. I'm not sure how Shane's session will hit my stomach after all this."

"Was it all weekend?"

He nodded. "And it's fine now. I'm feeling better."

"And yet you just told me that you didn't know that you can keep down food."

"Whatever," he muttered. "I'm just tired of being sick."

"Got it," she said. "Maybe I'll discuss the contents of that shake with Dennis."

"We already did that too," Zander replied. "It's all taken care of. It's just a matter of letting my stomach calm down. So I'm fine."

And he was obviously getting upset at this conversation. She nodded and tried backing out. "Well, I'll go get a coffee. Do you want me to pick you up one?" As soon as the words left her mouth, she realized it was the wrong thing to say. Without even needing to see or to hear a word from him, she added, "Never mind." And she was gone.

As she strode to the dining room, she found Dennis there and a few other people just milling about, getting coffee. She walked over and asked Dennis, "He had a bad weekend, *huh*?"

Dennis nodded. "Honestly, I think it's because you were gone. He didn't know that you weren't here. He kept looking for you."

She winced at that. "It would have been such a simple thing to let him know," she noted. "I keep forgetting that we have a life out of here and that they don't and that they don't necessarily think about the fact that we aren't always here."

"And I think he cares a little bit more than maybe is good for him, or you, considering I haven't seen any sign that this is a relationship that you're looking to take any further. So maybe he just needs to back off a little bit."

She frowned at Dennis. "I really like him," she shared, "but I don't think he is ready for anything."

"Well, I wouldn't suggest you tell him that," said a man from behind her. "Because these guys don't like to think of themselves as being that far behind."

She turned to face Shane. "Do you really think that's what happened on the weekend?"

"I don't know if that was *all* of it," he clarified, "but it was definitely a large part of it, yes."

"Wow. ... I really like the guy. He's funny. He's cute. He's great company, but ..."

"*But* exactly," Shane declared, frowning. "Maybe we need you to back out of the scenario a little bit more."

"I'm happy to go either way to help him reach his goals here," she stated. "Yet I certainly don't want him to feel as if I'm rejecting him. I think rejection right now would be very tough. And honestly, I'm not rejecting him. I really like him," she confessed. "But he's here, he's injured, he's a patient. All kinds of things in my head tell me that's not something I should be going forward with. At least right now. He needs to heal, first and foremost."

Dennis nodded. "And you know something? A few years back we would have all agreed with you, but things have changed, and, with the wedding coming up, even more change is happening."

Nelly nodded. "He mentioned something about the wedding and how all that made him lonely in a way because he had seen so many relationships happen here but didn't think it would be something that could happen for him."

"The fact that he's even talking about it is really good though," Shane pointed out. "And I can see how he would be feeling pretty miserable and upset about it all, but still, it is something that we should keep an eye on."

"But let's not do anything about it right now," she suggested instantly. "As I said, I really do like him. I just didn't expect to see this happen. I'm not the kind of person who other people would, … would fall for."

At that, both men stared at her.

"What?" she asked. "I'm not trying to be … I don't know what you even call it," she muttered, trying to find the word and failing. "I'm just … I'm concerned about him."

"We all are," Dennis stated. "Yet, at the moment, I think the best thing we can do is give him the best way forward, whatever that means."

She nodded. "You guys decide then. I'm happy to do what needs to be done that is the best for Zander. Still, I would hate to even lose the relationship I do have with him. However, if it's for his own sake, then fine. I understand."

"Good," Shane agreed. "I'll talk to Dani about it, and we'll see how it goes for the next couple days."

And, with that, Nelly had to be content. She did plan to spend some time with him, knowing that it could come to an end, and he probably wouldn't understand. Still, at lunchtime, she walked into his room with a big sandwich, hoping to share it with him.

Zander looked at it, and his eyebrows shot up. "I'm not sure I can get that down," he noted cautiously.

"I figured we could share it," she suggested. "You eat half, and I eat half." He frowned. "Or do you not share?" she teased.

He rolled his eyes at that. "Of course I do, but obviously my stomach is a whole different story."

"And yet how did breakfast go down?" she asked.

"Breakfast was much better," he shared. "I guess I got upset over the weekend. I had no right to do it."

"And I'm sorry I wasn't here," she murmured, "particularly if you were struggling."

He laughed. "There are always struggles, and, when you think about it, you won't always be here anyway, so it doesn't matter."

"Maybe," she admitted, "but I should have told you. We've spent enough time together that it wouldn't have been too much to tell you that I would be gone for the weekend."

"Funny how I never really noticed people coming and going, until you were the one coming and going. As a resident here, going through rehab, I have workouts every day, whether the weekend or not. So time off wasn't really something I thought about or considered, even for you. And then, all of a sudden, I realized you were gone, and I guess I overstepped my bounds."

She sat down on the edge of the bed and looked at him. "And what does that mean?"

He grimaced. "I was … thinking that you were off with a boyfriend."

Her eyebrows shot up. So Shane was correct. She shook her head at that. "No, not only was I *not* off with a boy-friend, I was off with two girlfriends. I don't have a relationship right now, haven't had one in a while, and I'm definitely interested in making new friends."

He looked at her sharply.

She smiled and nodded. "So, let's start with half of a sandwich."

"Is that like half of an olive branch?"

"If you extend the other half, then yes."

He smiled at her. "Done."

ZANDER HAD TO smile for the rest of the day and kept on smiling for the next few days. Even Shane noticed it.

"Well, obviously you have something good happening in your life," Shane noted. "Care to share?"

Immediately Zander shook his head. "Nope, definitely not sharing."

At that, Shane's eyebrows shot up. "Oh, even more curious."

Zander glared at him. "No, nothing curious at all."

"That's interesting," Shane murmured. "Maybe I'll just ask Nelly."

At that, Zander's glare upped in wattage. "Or you could just *not* ask her," he snapped.

Shane chuckled. "Or I could *not*," he replied. "That's always an option too."

Zander studied him hesitantly to see if he was serious, but it seemed as if he was being sincere. "It would be appreciated if you didn't," he said.

"Good enough," Shane stated. "Still makes for a pretty interesting day though, doesn't it?"

"It makes for something very interesting," he muttered. Then he shrugged and added, "Whatever, she's a nice lady."

"She is. She is, indeed. And considering that a wedding is in the air, I wouldn't be at all surprised if a whole lot more relationships happen around this place," he shared, with a chuckle. "Nothing quite like a wedding to stir things up."

Zander nodded at that. "Honestly, somebody had to tell me what was going on because I wasn't even aware of how this, ... what *all this* was about," he admitted. "I certainly heard lots of chittering and chattering, but I wasn't aware it was about Dani and her wedding, not until somebody sat me down and told me about it."

"Yep," Shane confirmed, "and we've been waiting for this for a long time. Everybody thought they should have gotten married earlier, but they wanted to wait until he was done with school."

"I can understand that to a certain extent, but, wow, what if something had happened, and you lost all those years?"

"They were together every moment that they could be," Shane explained. "Anyway, Aaron's just been gone to school a lot, so that didn't necessarily change anything."

"Good point," Zander noted. "Just because you're not married legally doesn't mean that you don't appreciate and spend every moment of your time with that special person. And, for the longest time, I never thought I would ever get married," he admitted. "I have to admit, seeing all this wedding planning stuff has kind of, … well, it certainly makes you think, doesn't it?"

"It certainly does," Shane agreed. "And it's something my partner and I are discussing. However, this is Dani's special day, and we all want it to go off perfectly."

Zander laughed at that and thought about it over the next day, as he drank his green drinks and went through his therapy and went on to working with Shane and doing everything that needed to be done. Because Dani's wedding did make Zander think, and it was all about Dani having her day. However, as soon as Dani had her day, Zander bet there would be a whole rash of other weddings happening too. He mentioned it to Nelly when he met her for lunch several days later.

She laughed. "I had the same thought. I think a lot of people are just waiting for Dani to get through the process and to have her special day. Everybody seems to be waiting for that. However, before her relationship with Aaron, who was one of the first patients here, Hathaway House always had this rule about no fraternizing with the patients," she shared in a teasing tone.

"Ha." Zander smiled. "You weren't here back then, so how would you know?"

"Believe me that I looked into it to see just what the rules were," she shared blithely, missing the expression on his face as she mentioned that. "And I was told quite clearly that it was okay now, but years ago? Well, apparently it was quite frowned upon."

"I would imagine in a lot of places it's still frowned up-on," Zander guessed.

"Yes, I'm sure it is, but things are a whole lot different here."

"Hathaway House is really different on many levels," he murmured. "I didn't really believe it at first. I'd heard so much about this place, and that's why I applied, but I didn't really know if it was as good as all the hype until Xavier came through here, and he kept me posted on how he was doing. That's when I realized that, one way or another, I had to get here, and I had to have this same type of miracle for myself."

"And you'll get it," she declared. "We just need you to build and to gain at a slower pace than Xavier did."

Zander nodded at that comment. "Very different consti-tutions, very different injuries, very different everything," he admitted. "And I think I'm calmer now about the whole thing, I just hadn't really realized—" And then he fell silent.

"Hadn't really realized what?" she asked. "You can't just leave it like that."

He chuckled. "No, it's probably not fair, yet it feels weird to say anything."

"Now you really have to fill that in," she stated curious-ly.

He shrugged. "I just really never thought about my future, other than how I would get through to the next meal or to the next day," he shared. "Now it feels very different. It feels as if I have to look forward in a completely different way."

"I don't know that *have to* is true in any way," she pointed out. "If you're ready to start looking at your future, then sure, fly at it," she stated, "but to say *have to* doesn't really fit, does it?"

He frowned as he thought about it. "Maybe not, but it does feel that way."

"Okay then, go with that."

He chuckled. "You mean, if I feel like I *have to*, then just go with it?" he teased. "I guess everything here is a case of handling each day, day-to-day."

"It is absolutely day-to-day," she stated, "for me too. My patient roster goes up and down on a daily basis. And sometimes I think something should happen, but then the doctors step in and change something. So what I think will happen doesn't necessarily happen, and things blow up from there," she said, with a shrug. "It's a learning curve, and I'm okay with that because I'm learning too."

"And that's very important," Zander noted. "And the fact that you're learning and growing and improving your own skills, I think that's also huge."

"It is," she murmured. "And I don't really know what I'll find on a day-to-day basis, but I'm okay with that."

"Good," he said, with a smile. "Sounds as if you've got it together."

She chuckled. "And, if that's what I sound like," she

muttered, "man, do I need to change how I speak because I do not have it together in any way." He looked at her in surprise. She shrugged. "Just like everybody else here, I'm learning to be a better person. I'm learning better ways to respond to patients, learning to modulate my voice if something doesn't go my way," she acknowledged, with a laugh.

"We all try to do our best, but it's not that easy. We're all living in a confined space, and sometimes it's a little hairy. And right now there may be an increase in a few short tempers, although I can't say anybody's short-tempered. Yet, as the wedding draws closer, there are more things to plan and more things to get done. A bunch of people are trying to do special events for both the bride and the groom—showers and things," she shared. "And, of course, everybody wants in on all of it." She gave him an eye roll. "I'm pretty sure Dani will be more than happy when this is over with."

"Of course she will," he agreed warmly. "And I'm sure she's enjoying every minute of it." And then he stopped and corrected himself. "Well, maybe not *every* minute of it, but she will enjoy the end result and the memories, especially when this is all over."

Nelly stared at him, nodding. "I think that's a really good way to look at it, even to look at your time here. You're building memories. And you'll take those memories with you, good ones, bad ones, ones that you had to stretch and grow yourself, ones that made you stop and wince because maybe you didn't do quite so much stretching and growing as you could have."

"Oh gosh," he muttered, with a groan. "I don't even want to think about those."

She gave him a fat grin. "Exactly. So I think those are

even more important sometimes, but, just as we're helping Dani build memories for her own experience here," she shared, "I think that's really important that she gets to have the experiences for later, for the memories down the road, when she's been married ten years and when she's got four or five little rug rats running around," she added, laughing.

"Oh, wow, I never even thought of that," Zander admitted, "but it could be her life, couldn't it? She and Aaron will probably have a growing family after this."

"Well, they've waited this long, so I would imagine so, yes," Nelly agreed. "But I haven't talked to her directly about it, so I have no clue. We're just happy that this is finally happening. I haven't been here all that long, so it's certainly not something that I'm in the know about. Yet I hear lots of people have felt this was a long time coming. And everybody's pretty excited," she shared.

"But it's not for a while yet."

"No, not for a while, but honestly, that *not for a while* part will happen so fast that *not for a while* will become *Oh, it's tomorrow.*"

He burst out laughing and then nodded. "You could be right."

"Oh, don't you worry," she stated. "It'll be calm, calm, calm, and then it'll be chaos."

"Hey, sometimes it feels as if it's chaotic here now," he pointed out, laughing.

And she agreed. "But nothing compared to what'll happen leading up to the wedding," she declared. "I suspect that, right before the wedding, all kinds of things will get really dicey, as we work with new patients, while everybody's working and planning on things in the background. Then, all of a sudden, this utter calm will descend on us all because it'll all be done, with everything taken care of, and then it's just fun times."

"And we're all here as part of it?" he asked. "Right?"

She nodded. "My understanding is absolutely everybody is invited as part of the festivities, with the wedding outside. Anybody who's capable of attending can attend. And those who don't want to have anything to do with it don't have to. They can stay in their rooms."

"I wonder if anybody will stay in their room," he pondered.

"It may bring up a lot of heartache for those people who may not have a family anymore," she noted. "And there could very well be heartache for those who have family but aren't here with them."

"Oh, I never thought of that either." Zander stared at her. "You're right. That could be emotionally difficult."

"Well, we're prepared—or are preparing for all of it," she shared, with a smile. "So there'll be both good and bad reactions, even to a wedding."

"Right, so the important thing is that everybody feels as welcome as they can be."

She looked at him and grinned. "See? You're already getting the hang of this."

He rolled his eyes. "I don't know how much of a hang of any of this I'm getting," he acknowledged, "but I am sleeping a bit better."

"And sleeping better is how we want to start," she stated. "As soon as you can sleep better, then waking up feeling better is the next step."

He snorted. "I'm not sure about that, but I feel as if it's starting."

"Good." She nodded. "Then we'll get you through the

day where it's not so exhausting to do one thing but instead you do a couple things, and then it just moves on from there."

He smiled at that. "You make it sound so easy."

"And it definitely isn't," she conceded. "I know that. Been there, done that, and it's not. I see it happen time and time again."

Chapter 6

N ELLY COULDN'T STOP thinking about Dani's wedding and all the plans that were being made. It was exciting, and it was fun, mostly because everybody wanted it to be a special day for Dani. However, Dani was starting to look a little frazzled the closer and closer she got to the date.

When she collapsed into a seat in Nelly's office one day several weeks later, Dani announced, "I'm taking time out from wedding plans." She looked at the door behind her. "If anybody comes to that door with a question, shoot them."

At that, Nelly burst out laughing. "Wow. I wondered when the stress would hit you."

"It hit me a while ago," she admitted. "Who knew that planning a wedding would be so stressful?"

"Oh, I think a lot of people knew, but were hoping that they could make it a little bit less stressful for you."

"And they are," she grumbled. "So many people are involved in this. It just sometimes feels as if it's too much."

"I think that's a normal way to feel," Nelly replied, with a smile, "but you're doing great."

Dani rolled her eyes at that. "Sounds like more cheerleader stuff to me."

"Hey, do you need cheerleading stuff? Because you know I got that down pat pretty well."

Dani chuckled. "By the way, how are things between

you and Zander?"

Her eyebrows shot up. "What do you know about me and Zander?"

"Are you kidding, in this place?" she scoffed. "I know probably as much as you do." And then she burst out laughing. "No, I don't mean that obviously, but you do understand that you can't keep any secrets here, right?"

"Nope, we sure can't. That's why I'm glad you decided to do the wedding thing for everybody because everybody wants to be a part of it, and they all want to make it special for you."

At that, Dani's expression softened. "It's appreciated, and I realize that I'm not part of an island here," she shared. "It's just so amazing that everybody wants to be involved. It's also just so mind-blowing that so much of this is happening right now. I've waited a long time."

"You have, indeed." Nelly smiled. "There's so much more out there for you, and I'm so thrilled."

"So many of us are involved in all these preparations," Dani noted, "that sometimes I forget that you haven't been here all that long."

"No, not that long," Nelly replied, "but, hey, I am more than happy to do my part in all this."

Dani chuckled. "Nobody should have to do their part in any of it. It's supposed to be on a volunteer basis, after work hours." And then she gave an eye roll at that. "No way to make that happen though."

"Nope, not at all," Nelly agreed. "So take it with grace and realize everybody is just thrilled to be a part of it at all."

She nodded. "And that's important too," she murmured. "Everybody is so good-hearted here, and they're doing everything they can for me. … Still, I just want it over with."

"Not happening," Nelly declared cheerfully. "There's a reason for the whole wedding production thing."

"Yeah, so *everybody else* feels good." Dani hopped up to her feet and added, "Okay, I've hidden long enough. Now I'm back at it." And, with that, she bustled back out again.

Nelly sat for a long time, smiling over Dani's antics. It had to be stressful to deal with so many different personalities and with so many needs of a large wedding. Meanwhile, everybody was still trying to do their best to make Hathaway House run perfectly because anything less was letting Dani down. And nobody was willing to do that. Something about that woman not only had everybody wanting to do the best for her, but also wanting to do the best they can do. Period.

Dani was a special person, who had managed to create so much loyalty. And Nelly was an equal part of that. She was just as happy to be loyal and to work hard at this place as anybody else, and she hoped that it would be pretty obvious, at least soon enough. For Dani, it was just a case of getting her through all this and keeping her sanity. Then she would have her first extended holiday in a very long time, as she and Aaron headed off on a honeymoon.

Nelly hadn't even asked what their plans were for the honeymoon, she'd heard whispers about Bali so figured that maybe Dani didn't even know. All Nelly knew was that it was pretty obvious that whatever was going on was special. And, for that, Nelly was overjoyed for Dani's part. Now if only they could get through all the rest of what needed to happen as well, because Nelly would like to see the wedding go off without a hitch. Then, hey, as soon as Dani was married, they would see others getting married too.

Zander was right. It did start you thinking about what else you wanted in life and what you would do to get it and at what point in time it was important enough to really chase after it. She didn't want to sit and spend her days waiting for life to happen, not if she could do something to make it happen herself.

But she wasn't even sure what she was ready for anymore. Just so much in her world had her stopping to think, *What was happening? What would be happening, and what was the right thing to happen?* And yet still, she didn't have a relationship that was tested and ready to go the distance. She did have somebody who she thought might be interested in taking that test run, though. Yet he certainly wasn't at that point yet.

However, if ever anybody needed to learn that something was out there for him, it was Zander. That guy had a lot going for him. He just didn't believe it—or didn't believe in himself. But he was getting there. Every day he was getting a little bit better, and she was delighted to be part of the journey. To see him now, to see him even compared to where he'd been when he had first arrived, was to see progress, massive progress, and, for that, she was absolutely ecstatic. He was a good guy. One of those good ones about whom your mom would have said, *Hang on to him.*

As Nelly considered that, she nodded slowly. She really did need to hang on to him. She just didn't know if he was ready for somebody to be interested in him. He never mentioned anything about it, just made slight comments about other people getting married. She wasn't even sure how he felt about marriage. She pondered that for the next couple days.

Finally one day he asked her, "So what's occupying your mind so much these days?"

She smiled at him. "Dani's wedding."

"Okay, that makes sense. What about it?" He lifted his coffee cup for a sip, peering over the rim at her.

"Just wondering how I felt about marriage," she stated simply.

He looked at her in surprise. "And here I figured you were the kind to turn around and get married and have your perfect 2.5 kids."

"There's no such thing as the perfect 2.5 kids," she declared, chuckling. "I gather the stats say that the average family has two point something kids," she admitted. "I never quite figured out how that was supposed to ever work out in reality, but not everybody is cut out for marriage."

"You are," he stated.

She looked over at him, one eyebrow raised. "Not so sure about that. I've never gotten that far, and I guess I always assumed that I would get married at one point in time, but it's not happened yet. I wasn't thinking that I had to rush into it or was even worrying about missing it. Yet now, watching the excitement with Dani's wedding—and the chaos—it makes you think. *How do I feel about it? How, … how does any of it fit into my life?*"

"Did you get any answers?" he asked.

She shook her head. "No, I really didn't. I'm still thinking about it all. What about you?" she asked.

"Before … I always figured I would get married—somewhere along the line when I was ready to settle down. The accident pushed that aside," he shared simply.

"Why?"

"When you get badly hurt, and you see everybody with supportive families around you, it becomes something that you desperately want so that you're not alone. At which point you realize that now that you don't have a family already, your chances of ever getting one are pretty slim."

"I don't know that that's true," she pointed out. "What I've seen and heard about the relationships that have started at Hathaway tells me that's wrong."

He shrugged. "I'm not sure that it's *not* true either," he countered. "Yet I get it. I see Xavier. I see Dani. I see Shane and his partner, plus Robin from downstairs, even Stan. Everybody seems to be paired up. I don't know how many of them came about because of this place, and that's not really the issue. It's just it makes you think about it. It also makes you wonder if thinking about it does any good. Sometimes I fear it can lead to more depression."

She nodded. "I guess I hadn't considered that either. It's like some never-ending negative talk, and that is destructive."

"That's because Hathaway House is geared to healing the whole body, but people like you, you're not dealing with major health issues. Whereas I could end up being hospitalized again. That's hardly a life for anybody to look forward to who was hooked up with me. Even if I did end up with children—which I always thought I would have—it's hardly a life for the woman and the children in my life."

"Ah, so you're focusing on the negative."

He glared at her. "Hardly," he snapped.

She winced. "Look. I didn't mean it as a criticism." But it was obvious that their conversation had slid south. "Let's just change the subject," she suggested.

He looked over at her and shrugged. "Sure, whatever."

She knew it was a touchy subject to begin with, and she didn't know why she'd pushed it. And she hadn't, not really. It's just he had asked her, and she'd told him and yet hadn't been able to question him further about his own thoughts on it. Because she did want to know his thoughts. She did want to know what his thoughts were on it all.

She liked him—more than *liked*—to be honest. They definitely had a rapport between them, but that didn't mean that they had anything close to something that would be sustainable. And, with that thought, she moved on, trying to keep the conversation light and out of any touchy zones.

WHEN NELLY GOT up the next morning and went in to work, she checked with the night nurse to see how Zander's night had been. Seemed it was not so good.

She frowned at that, wondering what was going on. Had she upset him the previous night? That would upset her if she had, and it would also give more weight to pulling back slightly. Frowning at all the thoughts going through her head, she headed to the kitchen to get his green drink and a half-dozen other green drinks for various patients who were up at this hour already.

As she walked into the kitchen, Dennis noted, "Well, that frown doesn't look very good."

She shrugged and replied, "I didn't even realize I was frowning."

"Also not good," Dennis said. "What's up?"

"Zander had a bad night last night, and I'm not too sure why or how come."

"They happen," he murmured, "and more often than you think."

She sighed. "I'm sure you're right. It's just not something that I still have any understanding about: the whys or the whens. I get word of a bad night, and I start trying to find a cause."

"There is a cause, but it's something that we have to check into first."

"You're right. It could be nothing."

"And it could be something," he declared cheerfully. "You never really know what is going on with people around here. The thing that you do find out very quickly is some of them are deep, and some of their problems are even deeper."

"Meaning?" she asked in confusion.

"Meaning that it takes time for some of the issues to surface. Now maybe you had a discussion with him, and it was completely unrelated, but it triggered something that was related," he shared, with a shrug. "Either way, it's important that it comes out and that it's dealt with," Dennis shared, "even though sometimes it's not that easy. I'll know more when I talk to him."

"You're correct there," she agreed, pondering it. "I'll see as soon as I get in his room and find out just how his night was."

He nodded. "Just don't push it. If he's touchy, let him be touchy. It usually means something's working its way through his brain."

She chuckled at that. "He has a pretty impressive brain. So, if something's working through there, it could take some time."

"Exactly," he agreed. "And that's the trick. Understand that it will take time."

She nodded. "Right, and don't take it personally."

"Never," he noted. "It's amazing just how much stuff does require time for each individual to sort out the mess in their heads and in their hearts."

And, with that, she grabbed the green drinks as Dennis handed them over, loading them up on her wheeled cart, and started delivering them to all the respective patients. By the time she got down to the last one—which, of course, she had saved as Zander's—she walked over to his room and knocked. When she got no answer, she hesitated and then knocked again a little firmer.

A sleepy-sounding Zander called her to come in.

She opened the door, stuck her head around the opening, and greeted him. "Hey. I wasn't sure if you were awake or not."

"Well, I wasn't," he replied, "but I am now."

She winced at that. "It is time for your green drink."

"Yeah, let's never *not* get that down on time," he muttered in a wry tone, as he shifted in the bed, rubbing his eyes. "I didn't have a great night, so not moving as well as I would like."

"Any particular reason for the lack of sleep?" she asked.

He yawned, shaking his head. "No clue, but it would be nice to find out sometime how that would work," he added, "because, man, oh man, some days I think everything is great. Then I turn around, and it's as if nothing is great."

"Sorry," she said sympathetically, as she walked over to help him adjust his bed so he could sit up.

"I really could use another four or five hours of sleep."

"It was that bad?" she asked.

He nodded. "It was that bad."

"I'm pretty sure you are allowed to push back your program for a day or two, especially if you had a bad night, because I know they don't like you pushing too much."

He shrugged. "What's *too much* though?" he asked. "It feels like a cop-out if I don't go."

"Okay. Maybe just ask Shane what he would want you to do."

He pondered that and nodded. "That might not be a bad idea." He pulled up his e-tablet and sent Shane a message. And then he took a sip of the green drink and stared at it. "For the first time since beefing-up my green drink—and promptly throwing up that first one—I didn't even shudder getting this down," he noted.

Nelly frowned. "I'm not sure if that's good or bad."

"That's because I've been putting on a good face."

"That's good, interrupting your usual frowns," she quipped. "But what shudders? I haven't seen any."

He rolled his eyes at that. "It means I'm getting used to the *new improved* green drink. It's not the easiest thing to get used to it. You keep changing the formula, so I never really know what it'll taste like each time."

"Since you've got lots of them coming," she noted, "the easiest you can make it on yourself, the better."

He nodded. "I get it. … I really do."

"Do you really hate it now? You really enjoyed that first one." It bothered her to think he'd been hiding his true reaction from her.

"No, I don't hate it, but neither do I particularly enjoy it. Although on a day like today," he pointed out, "it's probably even more necessary."

She frowned at him, seeing some of the pallor in his face. "Even if you don't hear from Shane, I'm clearing your schedule right now."

He looked at her in surprise. "What do you mean?"

"I don't like the way you look," she stated bluntly. "It's more than fatigue right now. Maybe you've overdone something."

He just stared at her and shrugged. "Just too many unruly thoughts. Nothing bad."

"Maybe not, but it's had an effect, and not a good one." She waited while he finished his green drink and added, "I'll be back in a little bit with your second round."

"And what do I tell Shane?" he asked her.

"I'll find Shane and tell him myself," she replied. "So don't you worry." And, with that, she disappeared. She would find Shane and fast because she didn't like anything about Zander's appearance this morning. As she walked toward Shane's office, he popped his head out, still talking to somebody in the room behind him. When he saw her, he asked, "Are you looking for me?"

She nodded. "Zander doesn't look good this morning. I'm not sure what's going on. He told me that he had a terrible night, overthinking things, but he looks bad."

"*Bad*-bad?"

She shrugged. "I don't know what that even means anymore," she admitted. "But I already cleared his schedule and told Zander to just stay in bed and rest."

"That's bad," Shane noted. "I'll head off and talk to him myself then."

Nelly nodded. "Let me know if he's okay."

"You think he's just had a relapse?" Shane asked, as he motioned at the hallway. "Come on. I'll walk you back to your office."

"I'm not sure what it is," she said. "He just looks … I don't know." She shrugged. "I can't explain it."

"Not a problem," Shane replied. "And you're right. Good call if he's tired and worn out. No way we can stress his body by doing more today. And sometimes it'll just be that way. We won't see a whole lot of progress for a while, and then hopefully his system will calm down, and we'll see a nice period in there, where we can make some progress."

"And I'm afraid that, without the progress, he'll get quite depressed too."

"He's been here almost what, two months?" he asked, frowning.

"Something like that, maybe a bit longer."

"In his case, his immune system was pretty shot, and I don't want him to get sick."

"I'm afraid that might already be too late," she muttered, with a sigh. "I just wish I knew if there was any way to ward off him getting worse."

"There is," Shane declared bluntly. "Lots of rest, bed rest, green drinks, and double up on the nutrition. I'll talk to the kitchen about it too, but first I'll go talk to Zander." And, with that, Shane headed to Zander's room.

ZANDER LAID UNDER the covers, hearing the voices going up and down the hallway, but they were distant, as if far off. When a knock came on his door, he went to call out, but it opened almost immediately, and someone poked their head around the corner. Zander popped his head up from the blanket and looked to see who was here. "I'm fine," he said to Shane.

Shane stepped in, took one look at him, and replied, "Sure you are. You're under the covers because you feel so healthy."

Zander shrugged. "I dunno. I just had a bad night. I just didn't feel quite myself."

"Good to know," Shane stated, "and you need to stay in bed. So you did the right thing."

"I don't know about the right thing," Zander admitted.

"I feel as if anytime I sneeze that everybody'll overreact."

"Because every time you sneeze, everybody will *react*," Shane clarified. "The overreacting part with you is hardly overreacting."

Zander nodded. "I was really hoping that I would be doing better by now."

"Was yesterday too much?"

"I don't think so," he murmured, "but I did wake up tired." At that, he shivered visibly.

Shane walked closer and asked, "How about a hot drink?"

"Sure. I had my greens already."

"A lot more of them are coming too," Shane pointed out. "I'll be back in a little bit." And, with that, he headed to the kitchen, presumably.

Zander curled up on the bed and closed his eyes. He didn't tell Shane that his night had been fraught with nightmares. The same accident that broke his ribs, which punctured his lungs, and dealt a blow to the rest of his body just replayed over and over and over again. He didn't know whether that was a result of something he ate or just some of the work he was doing with the shrink or just what. Yet it seemed as if the images were more colorful and brighter and stronger.

So every time he closed his eyes, he heard and saw all the sounds and sights of vehicles and gunfire and blasts and crying in pain. Stuff that he didn't want to ever deal with again, and yet it seemed as if he was stuck in this never-ending loop of a nightmare.

He closed his eyes and curled up under the blankets, grateful for a day on his own. And that was stupid because he was here to improve. Yet right now there just didn't seem to be any improvement possible. When he heard a sound in his room again, he opened his eyes to see Shane walking into his room with a tray. Zander shuffled to sit up.

Shane shook his head. "Just stay where you are." He put down the tray and then picked up the remote to the hospital bed and worked it so Zander was sitting up a little bit. Shane turned to face him and asked, "Did you get any sleep last night?"

"Not much," he murmured. "I tried hard."

"Of course you did, but sometimes life doesn't always go the way we want it to."

"That's very true."

"And is something being triggered?"

"Lots of things are being triggered, but most of it's nightmares," he admitted. "I wondered how much of it may have had something to do with my shrink therapy sessions."

Shane nodded. "That happens more often than we ever expect."

"I don't get how that works. We lock down all this stuff and tuck it away, trying to move on with our life. Then somebody says something to trigger it all again, and supposedly it's a good thing bringing up all this stuff?"

"Yes, because locking it down doesn't help," Shane murmured. "Confronting it and letting it go? Now that's a different story."

"How do you let it go?" he asked, staring at him. "The memories of my accident will be with me for life."

"Maybe, but, as we build up your immune system and get you stronger and have a little bit more muscle to handle some of this," Shane explained, "then you'll find it easier to deal with more and more of the mental health issues. I always like to believe that the body can handle everything that it's got going on," he shared, "but the truth of the matter is, sometimes the body can handle it. Sometimes the mind can handle it. Sometimes the heart can handle it, but to get all three to handle everything all at once? That's a miracle trick that we can't always do."

At that, Zander nodded. "I would agree with that. Sometimes it just seems to be too much."

"There's no doubt about it. Sometimes it definitely is but not this time." Zander frowned at him. Shane shrugged and declared, "We won't accept that it is too much. A lot is going on in your world, but you can handle it."

"I would like to think so, but I'm not so sure sometimes."

"I wouldn't worry about it," Shane suggested. "Although we've come a long way, still there's been a lot that we haven't had a chance to get to yet."

"And yet I thought maybe I was past this. I have been feeling much better. And, when you do a lot, it's like ten steps forward and two back."

"But," Shane clarified, "if the two back is what we're really dealing with, then, in theory, that's great because you're still eight ahead."

Zander stopped, thought about it, and nodded. "I guess, but it just seems—in so many ways—as if it's two forward and two back."

"Nope, not at all," Shane corrected. "I've seen lots of progress so far. It's just not enough for you to see it yet, and that's the sad part because you're the one who needs it the most in order to stay motivated enough to continue."

"Oh, I'm motivated," he stated. "I was just hoping to see progress faster."

"Everybody is," Shane said, with a knowing look. "Now

drink your new green drink while I'm here, to confirm you get it down," he added, with a smile. "And then I want you to have some of that hot soup."

"Good idea." Zander picked up the green drink, took a sip, and winced. "Wow, this is really … green."

"It is," Shane agreed, "and I'm a little concerned about your stomach handling some of this, but let's do the best we can."

"I can get half of it down before the soup and then try some soup and see if that'll help get some more down." And, working it slowly, Zander managed to get to the end of both the soup and the green drink. Then he laid his head back down. "Now I'm really tired."

"And that's fine. Your body has a lot of healing going on," Shane pointed out. "You're off today, possibly tomorrow."

"Tomorrow's Saturday," he said, his eyes opening.

"Right, but we run shifts throughout the weekend here. You need a day off sometime," he noted. "Sometimes we schedule them in for that reason alone," he shared. "We hadn't in your case, because so far, the schedule's been pretty light."

"Apparently *light* doesn't mean the same thing to me," he murmured. "That just adds to my feeling of, *Hey, I'm not doing enough.*"

"Don't ever feel that way," Shane replied. "You cannot compare yourself to everybody else."

"Too late," he muttered.

"And definitely not to your friends because your friends always seem to be getting everything better, faster, stronger than you. But they may not feel the same way."

His eyes flew open, and he stared at Shane. "Wow, I

guess you really have heard it all."

Shane smiled. "I've certainly heard enough, and I've seen enough to understand how the psyche works in instances like this. The criticism and the judgment and the comparisons are all a one-way street to disaster, so don't go there," he murmured. "You'll do just fine. If it takes you a month longer, it takes you a month longer. This is not a race. You don't have any restriction on your time frame here, so you'll do just fine."

After a moment of silence, Zander nodded. "Thank you for that."

Shane shook his head. "No need to thank me. I'm not trying to tell you that just so you feel better. I'm telling you that because it's the truth. That is the one thing I will always guarantee you. I will always tell you the truth, whether you like it or not. If you're shirking your responsibilities or you're not doing enough to get where you need to go, I will be the one to tell you. However, right now, that's not part of this deal." He grinned.

"I need you to get onto your feet, better, stronger, faster than the others could even have imagined, just for your own sake," he said, "but not to make you feel better. It's so that you see progress and so that you continue to build up your body. The more you do, then the more you can do. It's like an avalanche at that point in time. You're just not there yet, but you will be." And, with that, Shane grabbed the tray and was gone.

Not a whole lot Zander could do but close his eyes and smile because, even if it might be nice to get fed lies to feel better for the moment, the truth counted in the long run. And, of all the things that he'd seen so far, everybody appeared to come from a point of truth, whether it was theirs or his, but it always seemed to work out for the best to make him feel as if he was doing something right, somewhere along the line.

Sure enough, if it took another week or two—or three or four maybe—before he saw enough progress to make him happy, even to know that they weren't giving up on him, well, that was huge already. He closed his eyes at that point, took a deep sigh, and fell asleep again.

Chapter 7

OR THE NEXT few days Nelly kept a close eye on Zander, something she seemed to have gotten into a habit of doing.

By the fourth day, when she walked in for the fourth time that morning alone, he sighed and muttered, "I'm fine, you know?" She frowned at him, but he nodded. "I get it. You care, and you're worried, but I am fine."

She crossed her arms over her chest, a little upset that she'd been quite so transparent, but he was right. So there was little to refute.

He grinned at her. "And, yes, it's great that you care. Don't worry. I'm not upset at all. It's nice to know that everybody here is so concerned, but you all have to just lay off a little bit. I'm starting to feel as if I can't even go to the bathroom without three others in the room."

"And yet you're sure that you're okay?" she asked, looking for signs of the same fatigue that she had seen before.

"I'm fine," he repeated, "feeling much better, much stronger. I just needed a day or two of rest."

"Which is interesting," she noted, "because you hadn't done very much."

"*Thanks*, I didn't need that reminder," he quipped.

She winced at that. "Sorry. I promise that I'll lay off."

"Good, but while you're here …"

"What do you need?" she asked.

"Actually I was hoping to go to the dining room and have an early lunch," he said. "I'm really hungry."

"If you're hungry, we're going." She walked over to his wheelchair and brought it closer.

He added, "But I'm wheeling myself."

She hesitated, but seeing the look on his face, she conceded, "Fine, be independent and all that."

He burst out laughing. "That's what I'm supposed to be, aren't I?"

"Absolutely," she agreed, with a big grin. "It's just we try to help, but, at some point, the help becomes more of a hindrance."

"I'm doing much better. I even had a minor workout with Shane this morning."

"Good," she said. "I hadn't realized you were back to that."

"Yep, just a little bit, just working myself back in again. I haven't been vomiting, haven't had any fever or any adverse reaction," he shared. "So I'll say everything's doing just fine right now."

She beamed. "I'm really glad to hear that."

As they moved their way down toward the kitchen, he waved at a couple people and told Nelly, "You guys all have just so much heart that sometimes I wonder if you need to back off and not be so invested in everybody's life."

"It's not being invested in everybody's life," she clarified. "It's being enough invested to keep us caring and yet not so much invested that we can't let you go."

"Well, letting me go isn't exactly what I want," he replied, with a startled look.

She shrugged. "We have a lot of people who come for

rehab here, and we have to let them go when we've done our best with them. We don't always get an update. We often don't know what happens to anybody after they leave here. It's only the ones we have personal relationships with who care enough to tell us what they're up to," she explained. "It's like, … I guess it's like being a mom and realizing that, once you've let your children go, you don't have as much to do with them again."

As Zander wheeled himself to the dining room, she deliberately didn't say anything about the sweat beading on his forehead.

He stopped at the open door and muttered, "Okay."

She looked at him and asked, "*Okay*, what?" She kept her tone light, as if she didn't have a clue what was going on. When he glared at her, she shrugged. "You need to tell me what it is you want me to do. You're being very independent, and that's good. Yet …"

"Could you please help me the rest of the way?" he asked, followed by a deep sigh.

"Of course I can," she replied, her smile bright, stepping behind him as he wiped the sweat off his brow. She pushed him forward and saw Dennis cleaning behind the counter. She asked, "Hey, Dennis, when's lunch?"

He looked up, saw Zander, and smiled. "We're still getting prepped. Some of it's ready in the back though." He looked over at Zander. "Do you need food now?"

Zander shrugged. "I can wait a little bit. I don't want to be a bother."

"It's not a bother as long as you'll take whatever I give you."

"Ha, I haven't had anything from you guys yet that wasn't delightful." He waved a hand at the kitchen. "So bring it on."

Dennis looked over at her, raising an eyebrow.

"I'm fine for a bit," she replied. "This guy is hungry though."

"We'll fix that real fast," Dennis said, then disappeared into the back.

"What do you think I'll get?" he asked her in a contemplative tone.

"Knowing Dennis, it could be anything from throwing a steak on a grill to pasta to a salad or something simple, like a bowl of cereal."

"I could use a little more than that," he noted hesitantly.

"I wouldn't worry about getting cereal. They handle this stuff really well."

"They do, don't they?" He nodded. "I didn't think anybody would be open and agreeable to doing the stuff I throw at them, not without complaining."

"No point in complaining," she noted, with a smile. "Everybody here has one goal in mind, and that's to get everybody back on their feet and out to having a good life."

"And it's much appreciated." Zander smiled. "Sometimes it does feel as if we're a little bit lost here."

"I'm sure it often feels that way," she said, with a wry smile. "And not just for you, for all of us."

"Right," he muttered. "It's such a weird stage of life."

"Yes, it is, but that doesn't make it a bad stage." She pointed to the open dining room. "Where would you like to sit?"

He pointed to the table closest to the deck. "Just inside because I won't handle the heat well today at all."

"No, especially when you're still not feeling quite up to snuff."

"I thought I was, until I started rolling here."

"And that's fine," she added. "It's a good way to judge how your strength is."

"You mean, my *nonexistent* strength," he grumbled.

She worried at the slight bitterness in his tone. "You've come a long way," she murmured. "Hold the faith." She brought him up to the table, parked him there, and asked, "What about drinks? A coffee, water, what do you want?"

"Both would be great," he said. "I can come help."

"Nope, just stay where you are." She gave a wave of her hand. "At least then Dennis knows which table to set up your plate on."

As Zander sat here and waited, she returned with coffee, water, and cutlery for him. "What about you?" he asked. "I know it's too early for you to eat because it's not quite lunch yet, but—"

"I'm fine, and I'm happy to wait. Let's get you fed first."

When Dennis came back out, instead of a single plate he had a large platter.

She looked at him in surprise. "What have you got on there?"

He put it down in front of them. "A *sharesy* meal."

"A *sharesy* meal?" She'd never heard him use that term before. "I can wait, you know?"

"Maybe, but maybe not." He motioned at the platter now on the table.

She turned and saw the look of joy on Zander's face. "What is it?" she asked curiously, as she sat down beside him.

"It's loaded nachos," Zander declared, with a huge smile. He looked up at Dennis. "Man, this looks awesome."

"Think that'll hold you for a bit?"

"Oh, yeah." And he lifted up a corn chip with hot melted cheese, covered in hamburger and peppers and tomatoes.

"This looks delicious. It's a huge meal-full. Is this what's for lunch?"

"Some variation on that," Dennis replied. "I just made you a bigger version for the two of you now. Meanwhile, I have to get back into the kitchen." With that, he was gone.

Nelly stared at the platter in front of them and shook her head. "I don't think I've ever seen anything quite like this on the menu here."

"It's great," Zander mumbled, around his mouthful of food.

She chuckled. "If you say so." And she picked up a little bite cautiously because it was so hot.

But it was also so good. By the time she slowed down eating more of this, she realized just how hungry she was. And Zander wasn't even slowing down yet. She marveled at the kitchen's ability to bring out food like this and keep everybody happy while they were doing it. It really was something they should be proud of. As Nelly looked up, Dani walked in, a frown on her face, heading immediately for the coffee.

She saw them, smiled, walked over, and asked, "Hey, how are you guys doing?" Then she took one look at the platter in front and added, "Wow, loaded nachos. I hope that's for lunch for everyone."

"Dennis said, *Something like this*," Nelly murmured. "This guy needed food, so we came down early."

Dani nodded. "Good idea. If I had a few less things to organize in my life," she shared, "I would have tried an early lunch this morning too."

"How's the organizing going?" Nelly asked.

"I think we're just about there. Four more months may-be." She shook her head. "It doesn't seem to be anywhere near-enough time."

At that, Zander nodded. "I think for any big event you always feel that way. Then, on the last day, it all comes together."

"I'll hold you to that," Dani noted, with a smile, "because it doesn't seem as if it'll come together at all."

"It will," he stated, with a vote of confidence. "You've done an incredible job here at Hathaway House, and that's come together in ways that most people could never even imagine. So, for you, a wedding's simple."

"Wouldn't be so bad," she admitted, "but I keep getting notice of more people who want to attend."

"Have it outside where everybody can come and watch," Zander suggested. "Make life easy on yourself."

"And what if the weather doesn't cooperate?"

"Then everybody comes inside," he replied, with a smile, "or rent some tents. You could probably find one that goes over this massive deck here. That'll handle a lot of people."

She frowned at him, stared out at the deck, and raised one eyebrow. "Not a bad idea."

He chuckled. "I aim to please."

And, with that, Dani took her coffee and disappeared, muttering to herself again.

Nelly looked over at him and nodded. "That was good thinking."

"Dani's done so much for so many people," he pointed out. "So I can't imagine the wedding, outside of wedding nerves, being something that would beat her."

"Oh, I don't imagine it will," Nelly agreed, chuckling. "However, I do think this platter has beaten me."

He smiled at her. "That's all right. I'll take a hit for the team." And, with that, he proceeded to dig in even faster.

"Slow down, slow down. I was kidding."

"But you might change your mind," he noted, still with that big grin, "and I'm not sure I'll share anymore." With that, he went back to eating.

She stared in amusement at this guy who just yesterday could barely even get out of bed. Yet today he was tanking up on food like he'd lost fourteen meals. In actual fact he lost maybe one meal, and that's because he'd slept through it.

She smiled. "Now this," she muttered, "is good to see."

ZANDER WAS THANKFUL that his setback was the last one for a long time. As he slowly moved through the rehab program, he felt some of his positivity return as he saw, as Shane had promised, real progress. "Now that it's been a month since my last slowdown," he shared, "I'm realizing that I probably just overdid it, just did too much on a regular basis."

Shane nodded. "In a program like this, it's always hard to know at what point in time to call it quits. So it's important to listen to your body, to understand your own body, to know where you're comfortable with your workouts and what you can reasonably do long-term, day in and day out," Shane shared. "We're just happy to know that you're back on your feet again."

Zander smiled. "Particularly as things are heating up over the wedding."

"They sure are," he agreed, with a laugh. "You'll be here for it, as it's all coming down, so hopefully it won't bother you."

"Nope, not at all," Zander replied. "A lot of couples are

here. I'm wondering if any of those couples will take advantage of the whole wedding scenario and get married themselves."

"It's been mentioned, but everybody decided that they want Dani to have this day for herself. I'm sure there'll be a flurry of weddings after hers, me included," Shane added, with a boyish grin. "But it won't be the same kind of gala affair, that's for sure."

"Your partner doesn't want a big wedding?"

"Nope, neither of us do," he shared. "It'll be a fairly small event, with just family. We won't go through something like this, and we don't have a ton of time off, but we have enough to make it special." He nodded. "A lot of partners are all in the process of finalizing their relationships. So it's all good."

"I agree," Zander replied. "And yet, for me, it's an odd thing because I'm one of the single guys in here, without a relationship."

"And there are lots of them too," Shane noted. "You're not alone."

"I'm not sure that's something I want to have in common with others either," he replied humorously.

Shane chuckled. "I was alone for a long time myself, and I didn't worry about it, didn't push for it, because I figured it would happen when it happened. I wanted it to be somebody who saw me at my best and my worst."

"My worst is pretty bad," Zander muttered.

"No, it's not," Shane argued. "You've come a long way since you first arrived. Even when you got here, you weren't that bad. Weak, but that's to be expected. You had a series of heavy illnesses, and that can really take it out of you. But now you're doing so much better."

"And I think—for the first time in a long time—I agree with you," he admitted, with a smile. "It doesn't always work out that way. Yet I am feeling a lot more positive."

"Good. And, speaking of relationships, I thought you had a thing going."

"I would like to think so," he said. "However, I also know that, being here at work is a different thing for her versus for me."

"Meaning?"

"I guess I'm just afraid that—" He stopped, not sure how to explain it. "Just feels as if this is a very unnatural environment, and so any relationship that develops here might struggle out in the real world."

Shane frowned at him and shook his head. "And I think that's where you're very wrong. I think this is a microcosmic society, where everything is amplified. And so, if you can make it here, chances are good you can make it out there too, if not even better."

"I hadn't considered that," Zander muttered. "Still not sure I understand exactly what you mean by it."

"If you think about it, everything here is bigger, stronger, more real," he explained. "The accidents we can't walk away from, no makeup to hide the injuries." He added, "The internal scars are being exposed on a day-to-day basis as people go through therapy and training for the outside world. Therefore, if you can deal with your stuff in here, then everything out there—although it still must be dealt with—will be that much easier because you've dealt with it here first."

"Sure, but then adding in a relationship to that mix of healing and retraining, that's got to be hard."

"Maybe, but you've already gone through a lot of the

hard stuff here. So you don't have to worry about somebody being fake here because there's no room for that, no time for it. You see the person in crisis mode. When you see somebody in crisis mode, you see them as they truly are on the inside."

Shane reached up to brush a hand through his hair. "There's no way to hide it here. There's no closing a door and staying behind it for five days, coming out picture-perfect. It's dirty here. It's real here. It's gritty here. When people have great days, you have great days too. Yet, when they have bad days, believe me that you have to deal with those bad days. There's no putting it off or brushing it aside. There's no way you say, *Oh, not dealing with it today. I'll go off to work and ignore it until I get home again.* The days here are real and full and extreme, but, because of that, when you come up against something in the real world, where you already have this confront-the-problem basis to go on, I think a lot of relationships do exceptionally well because of that particular mind-set."

"I hadn't considered that." Zander stared at Shane in surprise. "I was thinking that, when you get out to the real world, there are all these other things to deal with that must be a factor too."

"Sure, but it's more a case of you and your partner against that world, trying to find ways to deal with it together, instead of you out there trying to fit into the new dating world and trying to figure out what you're supposed to present yourself as. Here you don't present yourself as anything but the real you. Here you are who you are, and there's no hiding from it." Shane stood up, with a knowing smile. "So you might want to remember that when you figure out whether it's worthwhile pursuing *her* or not."

Certainly Zander would think about Shane's words. As Shane ended their rehab session and headed toward the hallway, Zander asked, "What about all the thought processes about how we're broken while we're in here, and yet, as soon as we're out of here, isn't that a better way to have a relationship, when you're whole?"

"But what is the relationship you're trying to have?" Shane asked curiously. "Because, if you think about it, you're whole now. You might be damaged, but who you are is who you are, and you're not hiding anything here. When you leave here, you have the ability to mask so much of who you are, whether you think you're doing it or not. It becomes almost a self-preservation response out in that world, and that may not be good in any way, not for you or for someone you may meet and date out there." Shane pointed out.

"But here is this person, whoever you're talking about—and, yes, I have a pretty darn good idea who she is—she sees you as you are right now. You don't have to pretend to be better when you leave here. If you're better, that's great, but, at least, while you're here, she sees who you are and accepts who you are. And there isn't any waiting until you're better to become friends or waiting until you're better to go out on a date. You're already seeing that person on the inside, and that's worth a ton," Shane declared, "at least to me. I would rather take real and solid and know what I'm dealing with than to take a put-upon persona of what somebody thinks you should be like."

"Right, I would much rather have real," Zander agreed instantly.

"And that's what we do here," Shane noted. "We're all about the real. It doesn't always mean that you like what you see, but what you see is really what you get, and that's worth something." And, with that, Shane turned and walked out, leaving Zander alone to his crazy thoughts.

And, of course, Zander's thoughts immediately turned to Nelly, wondering just what he needed to do to see where she was at with this whole relationship thing. Because, as Shane had said, in the future Zander would move on from here. So the question was, what did he want to move on as, as himself or as something else? And for him it was always about being real. Did Nelly want the same thing? Did she like him? That was the real question.

Chapter 8

THE NEXT DAY, Nelly had just arrived, and Dani called out to her, asking her to come give an opinion about flowers. Nelly stepped in Dani's office and smiled at several displays. "Oh my gosh, those are gorgeous."

"I was thinking about the red ones," Dani noted hesitantly.

"If you're thinking about the red ones, then you do the red ones," Nelly stated. "Don't let anybody talk you out of doing what you want."

At that, Dani smiled. "You're such a great cheerleader."

"Hey, this is your wedding. You've waited a long time. You make it just how you want it."

"I would have been just as happy with a simple small wedding," she murmured.

"Sure, but it's not just me cheering you on right now," Nelly noted. "The whole center is."

"And I know that." She gave a small shrug. "It just seems, I don't know, maybe selfish in a way."

Nelly stopped and stared. "How on earth could picking red roses for your wedding be seen as selfish?"

"Because a lot of money is going into this wedding. Money that could be better spent on other things, like Hathaway House or the horses or the animals with Stan. That doesn't even begin to count the time spent by the volunteers, just to make this day *more special.*"

"I think a whole lot less time has been spent than you think," Nelly said, with a wry smile. "Almost everybody I know who is donating their time to make this happen are so happy to do it," she explained. "I know I am. I know that Ilse is. Everybody involved in this is. Plus, Bella got you a deal on the flowers from a local florist. There's the minister who, as you had already helped his son, is doing this for free."

Dani looked up, and her eyes glistened with tears. "I know. It's so wonderful. I have absolutely no reason to complain. Everybody is bending over backward to make this happen."

"When's Aaron coming in?"

"Not for another month. He's got two more practicums to go, and then he's done," she stated proudly.

"I'm really proud of him, and I don't even know him," Nelly said, with a laugh.

"You will certainly meet him soon, but he's been gone longer than he was ever here," she admitted. "It's been great though, seeing him follow his dream. Just so much has been happening with Aaron that it's hard not to feel proud of his accomplishments. And he's a huge reminder to everybody here that you can do whatever you want to do," she declared loyally. She gave a headshake. "Now, I'll focus on some work."

"You do that." Nelly laughed.

"Sorry, I didn't mean to distract you."

"Distract me all you want," she murmured. "As far as I'm concerned, nothing is better than helping you out for this special day." And, with that, Nelly went to her office.

She grabbed her file set aside for today and headed out

to meet the new patient who had just come in. There was always a turnover here, and sometimes it was faster than she expected, as people did better or as funding got cut or as the staff made needed changes. In this case a bed had come open because of a hospital visit that changed the course of the other patient's treatment. So now Nelly had a new patient to replace the former patient.

By the time Nelly was done with her morning rounds, it had been a busy morning, and she was good with that. She preferred busy over anything else. She walked down to check on Zander. When she entered his room to find it empty, she frowned at that but carried on through her day. She would catch up with him somewhere along the line. That's how it was here. Some days it worked, and some days it didn't for her and for him. By the time she wandered to his room again at the end of the day, there was still no sign of him.

Shane caught sight of her and said, "He's in the pool."

"Ah," she murmured, yet frowned.

"Zander wanted to go in. I figured, if he needed something different, something to boost him, he would benefit from the pool," he muttered. "Am I worried about him getting sick? Always. Still, we have to test the waters somewhat."

She nodded. "I get that. However, when he goes down, it seems to take him a long time to get back up again."

"It does, and that's sad. We're still beefing up his immunity, but it's much improved from where he was initially, when he first got here," Shane noted. "But, hey, he's doing pretty well. I was just there."

"Is he allowed to stay in?"

"One of the therapists is down there working with another patient, so she's keeping an eye on him," Shane replied. "So I'm off and heading to town. I'm on some secret wedding stuff missions," he whispered, with a laugh.

"You too, *huh?*" she said, with a big smile.

"I think we all are. Haven't had this much fun in a long time," he admitted, with a bright smile. "And Dani deserves it."

And that was a sentiment that Nelly heard over and over again because it was true. Dani did deserve it, and she'd worked so hard for everybody else's happiness that they were all more than eager to pitch in to make her wedding day something special.

Still unable to help herself, Nelly wandered down to take a look at Zander in the pool. As she stood at the edge of the water, it took him a long moment to realize she was here.

He broke through the water, saw her, and grinned. "Are you coming in?"

She shook her head. "I'm a bit on the tired side."

"The water would be good for you," he suggested. "I find it rejuvenates me completely."

"Maybe," she replied, still hesitating.

"If you come in now," he added, "we have time for a swim before dinner."

She laughed. "That's one of the reasons I came now, was to see if you were going to dinner tonight."

"Oh, you can bet I'm going," he declared. "No more missing meals for me."

"I'm also a little worried about your staying too long in there," she acknowledged, eyeing him carefully.

"You and everybody else," he teased. "I think you're about the fourth person to double-check on me."

She grinned. "Hey, we're all just one big happy family."

"According to everybody in this big happy family, they

all have secret plans for Dani's wedding," he noted. "It seems to be the event of the year."

"Probably of a lifetime," she claimed. "If we're honest, Dani's been waiting years for this."

"So I understand," he agreed, with a nod. At that, he shivered once. She frowned immediately. He raised a hand and muttered, "I know. I know. That means it's time to get out." He slowly made his way toward her. "Actually, you know what it means? It's time for the hot tub."

And, with a grin, he dashed into the hot tub—or at least as fast as he could make that dash happen.

She laughed as he sank under the hot water. "Now that makes more sense," she muttered. She walked over and sat down on the side of the hot tub and asked, "Will you be here long?"

"Why? Do you want to go somewhere?"

"No, I'll just go home, have a shower, and unwind from the day. Then I'll come back and collect you for dinner."

"I'll have to get changed for dinner too," he noted. "So what time is it roughly?"

"About 4:15, 4:20," she replied.

"So how about we meet for dinner at five?"

"You're on." She got up with a wave and walked away.

Zander called out, "Hey, is somebody doing a bridal shower for Dani?"

"Yes. All of that's been arranged. I got my invitation already."

"Good, I would hate to think something like that was getting missed."

"Not getting missed at all," she said. "It'll just roll into everything else that's happening around here."

He nodded. "Is there a wedding gift registry set up

somewhere too?" She frowned at him. He shrugged and asked. "Can't I contribute?"

"You absolutely can," she replied. "I'll have to find out who's handling that though."

"You do that. At least we still have enough time to order something."

"Depending on what she wants. Knowing her, she's asking for donations to Hathaway House."

He stared at her and nodded. "I bet she's done exactly that."

"We'll see." She gave him a smile, before leaving. As she walked back to her apartment, she realized that was exactly what Dani would have done. And yet Dani would still like some more personal things, even if just contributions toward a honeymoon. At that thought, Nelly frowned. She didn't know even what was going on with the honeymoon or many of the other plans. All she had heard was that Aaron had planned their honeymoon as a big surprise for Dani.

And, as Dani dealt with the ever-growing list of wedding guests, Nelly couldn't seem to keep up with all the added surprises coming up to celebrate Dani's and Aaron's big day.

SEVERAL DAYS LATER Zander slowly made his way to the dining room for lunch. He planned on meeting Nelly here if he could. When he looked up to see a strong and fit man striding toward him, Zander sighed as the newcomer got close. "Please tell me that you graduated from this place."

At that, the man stopped and laughed. "Absolutely I did." He reached out a hand and introduced himself. "I'm Aaron, by the way."

Zander smiled. "Ah, you're Dani's beau, aren't you?"

Aaron chuckled. "If that terminology is still used, then yes."

"I'm Zander."

"I stopped in just for the day," Aaron shared. "Nice to meet you."

"Hey, hang on a minute. A bunch of us want to figure out if we could do something special for Dani. We don't really have any idea what though."

He frowned at that. "I know that she would prefer charity donations to a personal gift."

"Sure, but that's not for her."

"And she would say this wedding isn't about her either," he added, laughing.

"Maybe. It would just be nice if we could do to something to make her personally happy."

Aaron nodded. "Let me think about it. I'll get back to you."

"Here's my phone number." Zander wrote it down on a piece of paper from his wallet and handed it over. "If you come up with anything, I know a bunch of us who want to do something special."

"Okay, but it would still have to be practical or something Dani believes in too."

"Right," Zander agreed. "Otherwise she'll feel as if it's a waste of money."

"Exactly," Aaron grinned. "At least you understand her."

"I know that her heart and soul's in this place," Zander shared. "So it's hard not to see that. As a beneficiary of all that she's learned and has put into Hathaway House, I can hardly complain."

At that, Aaron nodded. "I'm glad to see this place hasn't

changed, and it still comes from heart."

"How long since you've been here?" Zander asked.

"I was one of the original patients. Then I went back to school and became a vet," he explained, "so it's been several years ago since I was here. I'm now full-time in school, but that will all end very soon." He smiled. "I've got another month, not even, and then I'll be back in time to get ready for the wedding—and to leave on our honeymoon."

"Good enough. Let me know if you have any thoughts on a personal gift for Dani."

With that, he slowly moved to the buffet line and realized he was first in line. He shook his head as he looked over at Dennis. "I just met Aaron."

"Ah, nice guy."

"And apparently he was here, as a resident? Way back when?"

"He absolutely was here way back when," Dennis confirmed. "One of the first patients at Hathaway House."

"I asked him if he had any ideas of how we could do something special for Dani. I'm not sure how to make that happen."

"Sometimes there's some things we can do, and sometimes there are those things we can't do," he noted, with a shrug. "I think the fact that everybody wants to do something makes her feel good, but I don't think she particularly wants to see anybody go out of their way."

"Of course not." Zander rolled his eyes. "*Of course we don't want to go out of our way,*" he muttered sarcastically, "but surely there's something we can do."

At that, Robin stepped up behind him and interjected, "Hey, I have an idea for Dani."

"Oh yeah, what's that?" he asked.

She motioned to Dennis and added, "You might want to be part of this too."

At that, Dennis came around the counter and asked, "What's up?"

"You know Midnight."

"Yep, sure do, her horse."

"Well, she used to have another one, called Sunshine, a mare. Dani sold it years ago for funding to get Hathaway going. Anyway, the mare's just gone up on an auction block."

"I have heard her mention it a couple times over the years," Dennis noted, "but not recently."

"Her owners are retiring her. I really don't want to see her go to the wrong buyer, like some owner of a sausage plant."

"Oh good God." Dennis gasped, his eyes rounding in horror.

"She's a special mare to Dani. So I was thinking—"

"Yes, absolutely," Zander jumped in. "Tell me what you need for money, and I'll see what I can do to roust up some funds."

"It could be a couple thousand dollars," Robin guessed. "I don't really know."

"If that poor horse is being sold for meat, then hopefully Sunshine won't be that much at auction," Zander replied. "However, … as soon as anybody knows that we're interested in saving the animal's life, you know exactly what'll happen."

Robin nodded. "The price will jump, and I won't really care because it's for Dani. Still, it would be nice to get Sunshine at an affordable price."

"You're correct there," Dennis agreed. "Get as much

information as you can find. I'm sure all kinds of us will want to help out."

At that, Zander nodded. "But we also have to consider that, by giving her a gift, we're also giving her an expense."

Dennis nodded. "I hear you there, but I don't think that expense will particularly come into play in this instance."

"Maybe not. I just thought I should bring it up."

"It's a good point," Robin noted, with a smile. "Thankfully Dani operates as a charity, and there's a lot of money to help rescue animals, and this would definitely count. It would be the extra effort we expend to make it happen that would be more or less our gift."

"And I'm all for it," Zander declared. Dennis nodded.

And, with that, Robin disappeared.

Zander looked back at Dennis. "I never really saw a place that dedicated so much of its time and effort to humanitarian causes, even just to broken-down people like me."

"And you're not anywhere near as broken-down as you think you are," Dennis reminded him.

"I'll tell you one small bonus thing that I didn't realize was even a bonus until this morning when I woke up."

"Tell me," Dennis said. "We all need good news."

"I was in the pool last night," he began. "And I did catch a bit of a chill, but honestly, I feel fine today. So maybe, just maybe, my immunity is getting a little bit stronger."

"And that is definitely good news," Dennis declared. "I do like to hear that because the one thing we can't afford is to have you get sick again."

"I know. It sets everything back, doesn't it?"

"It really does, but, more than sets it back, it makes people think that you can't do anything, and that's not fair."

"No, and it doesn't feel fair in that sense either," Zander noted. "But I do appreciate the fact that people will at least let me go in the pool and try that out for a bit. I think that's important too."

"Very important in fact. You have to try. And each such achievement does feel as if it's a huge step forward. It's more than a huge step forward," he clarified. "It's massive." And, on that note, he pointed at Zander. "You'll get another green drink right now."

Zander groaned. "No, no, no, save me from the green drinks."

"Nope, you need it, especially after you went swimming yesterday," Dennis said. "We don't want that to creep up and hit you sideways tomorrow."

"Can it still?" he asked, staring at Dennis.

"Absolutely, so we'll nip that in the bud to confirm it doesn't." And he added, "You're first up for food, so I'll get you the green drink while you wait."

"I guess the food's not quite ready yet?"

"You get earlier and earlier every day," he pointed out, with a laugh. "Glad to see that appetite of yours is working hard."

"It so is," he agreed, as he rubbed his stomach. "It's amazing just how hungry I have been lately."

"But it's all good." And, with that, Dennis disappeared into the kitchen.

Aimless, Zander just turned to sit beside the buffet, as he stared around at the dining room, remembering just how many days he'd spent here not in great shape, versus even now, where he felt a lot more comfortable. It was good. It was all good. And, with a bright smile, he turned as Dennis rejoined him.

Zander's smile faltered at the size of the green drink. Then he shook his head. "Wow, I'm really glad you're trying to keep me alive," he teased, "because otherwise I might be thinking you're trying to kill me."

Dennis burst out laughing and said, "Drink up. This is great stuff."

And, with that prompting, Zander took a sip of his green drink. "I'll go sit on the deck and try to get this down."

"You do that," Dennis said. "By the time you're done, I'll have the first plate ready for you."

And, with that, Dennis disappeared into the kitchen yet again.

Chapter 9

T HE NEXT FEW days fell into a rhythm that was getting to be so easy. Nelly watched Zander work himself to the bone and then pick himself up, sometimes tired and sometimes not. Whenever she worried about something, he would listen before responding.

Each time he would sit back and grin and say, "I'm doing better. I'm doing much better."

"You are," she agreed. "I just don't want you to fall."

He nodded. "I get that, but I can't even express to you how much stronger I feel."

She hesitated because she needed to let him do his thing, but it was hard because she wasn't sure that he understood where his strength was at. So she often compromised and added, "Just a warning."

"I know. I know," he always said, and then he'd laugh. "Besides, everything's so crazy right now, with the wedding. You worry about that instead."

"It's not that bad," she muttered. "We're all doing our thing."

"Yeah, I was waiting to hear from Robin to see what was going on with Dani's personal gift."

"Right? She did contact the owner of the horse," Nelly murmured. "Yet still no word back."

"Well, the wedding is coming pretty fast," Zander noted.

"Not much time for a fallback gift—if this doesn't work out."

"It is, indeed, but it's not that bad. We still have time."

"Are people covering the flowers and stuff for her?"

"You don't think the horse is enough?"

"If there's a cost involved in the horse, absolutely," he said. "But I still suspect, with this many people wanting to show Dani how special she is, there'll be lots of room for other gifts."

Nelly stared off in the distance. "I know she got a special deal on the cost of the flowers, but for all the food involved?"

Zander frowned. "Maybe we can donate to that too."

"And I can talk to a couple of the people here who are organizing some of this. I'll see what they say," she added.

"A lot of people are here," Zander noted, "but we don't want people to feel that they have to donate. I've talked to a couple of the guys myself, and they want to. So, if the food bill is bothering her, let us help pick up that tab."

She stared at him and shrugged. "Maybe we should just put all collections into a big pot and cover what we can cover?"

"Sounds good," he said, with a smile.

AFTER NELLY LEFT, Zander looked at the remainder of his green drink, sighed, and tossed it back. If nothing else, he was feeling better and stronger. Although there were days where he woke up and didn't want to get out of bed, he had enough energy to get out of bed and to override that sense of being exhausted. There was a lot to be said for that too. As he smiled off in the distance, his phone rang. He looked down to see it was Aaron. "Hey, Aaron. I'm surprised to hear from you."

"There's been an awful lot of discussion going on about something for Dani," he replied.

"Absolutely. There has been multiple discussions here, from a horse that she used to have to maybe suggestions that we donate to the cost of the food, which seems to be bothering her too."

"Yeah, I hear you there, but something came up, and she'll be thrilled—when she realizes it—but it's a problem too."

"What's that?" Zander asked.

"We are getting the horse for her. And believe me that's in progress, but the owner won't let us pay."

At that, Zander stared down at his phone. "You mean he won't let her have the horse?" he asked in horror.

"Oh no, not that at all. Apparently his grandson went through Hathaway House. So, once he realized who the horse was for, he's now donating the horse to Dani as a wedding gift."

"Oh good God." Zander started to laugh. "And now I see what kind of problem you foresee. So many people are donating because she's done so much over the years that they all want to pitch in and do something for her. And now we have no idea what to spend our money on."

"Exactly. That's exactly what I would say," he agreed, with a laugh. "So, I will keep it in mind and will see if we can come up with anything else."

"Somebody suggested that we put all the contributions into one pot and cover as much of the expenses as possible, so that she doesn't feel as if anything has to go toward the wedding that she doesn't have the money for."

"And that's probably a good answer too," he admitted. "I have to admit, at this point in time, I'm a little bit out of the loop on a lot of the planning because I'm in exams," he shared, his voice a little distant. "And even now I have to run."

"Hey, thanks for the update, man."

"You too. Take care, and be strong for the wedding."

"Am I invited?" Zander asked, with a wry note.

"Everybody in Hathaway's invited," he stated. "Don't ever doubt that. And, if you have a plus one to bring, she's welcome too." And, with that, Aaron ended the call.

And Zander was left with that phrase that almost struck terror in his heart. *Plus one.* Was there anything worse than having to RSVP and to say you were coming alone?

Chapter 10

S EVERAL DAYS LATER Nelly watched from the hallway as Zander stood up slowly from the wheelchair, grabbed the crutches from Shane, and slowly made his way to her. She clapped a hand over her mouth, then exclaimed, "Oh my, look at you."

"I know. I'm taller than you expected, right?"

"Ha. You're also scrawnier than I expected," she pointed out.

He burst out laughing. "According to Shane, I put on eighteen pounds."

She turned to Shane for confirmation. He nodded. "Absolutely, and that is a good thing."

"How much of that is muscle and how much of that is chubs?" she asked, with a chuckle.

As Zander got closer, she reached out her arms, and he wrapped her up in a big hug. "Now that," he muttered, with a chuckle, "was well worth the work."

And she slowly turned him around and pointed. "Now back to Shane."

"What's the matter? Don't I get another hug?" he quipped.

"Yep, Shane will give you a hug at the other end," she teased.

He rolled his eyes at that and slowly moved forward. By

the time he got to Shane, Zander's grin was huge, but he hated how weak he felt.

"You've come a long way," Shane declared, "so don't ever knock it." He put him back in the wheelchair and declared, "Now, that'll do for today."

"That's good," Zander admitted. "I'm not sure I could have done any more."

"But you could have," Shane noted. "I want this now to become part of your workout."

"What part of my workout?" Zander asked.

"I want you to do this walk tonight before you go to bed, and then I want you to do it again in the morning before you come to see me."

"And you won't be there each time?" he asked, startled.

"Do I need to be there?" Shane asked, smirking at him.

"No, I, … I don't think so," Zander replied. "I'm pretty sure I can make do on my own."

"Good," Shane replied, "because I don't think you need me."

And, with that, Zander turned to face her with a huge grin.

"You know something?" she asked Zander, as Shane walked away. "I think you just graduated."

"Not from everything," Zander clarified, with a shake of his head. "But, hey, I'll take whatever I can for right now."

She nodded. "And now it's coffee time."

"Is it really?" Then he checked his watch. "And he sprung this on me at the end of the day."

"It's all good," she said. "You've been here four-plus months and look at you? You're back on your feet, walking with crutches so far, and you're gaining strength."

"He's got me doing weights now too," he added.

"That's because you need as much muscle as you can build right now," she noted, with a smile.

Zander shook his head at that. "The days are just racing by."

"I know. Have you put any thought into what you are doing after this?"

He nodded. "Lots of thought—but no answers."

She didn't want to push it, but she could see that he wasn't too bothered about it. "So presumably you have a plan of some kind."

"Absolutely." He chuckled. "I'm just not sure where I want to go with it."

"I think there are a lot of things you can do, but, hey, you still have time."

"I do have time," he agreed, "but, if nothing else, this shows me that I have such great progress happening, so then it must be time to start thinking about it."

She thought it was past time, but, hey, that's because she had dealt with so many people here already. Some came in absolutely struggling to find a way to make future plans, yet Zander seemed quite laissez-faire about it all. "You mentioned how your parents were in England. Is that where your sister is too?"

He just nodded, preoccupied with his thoughts.

"So no family close by, right?" she asked.

He again nodded. "Sure, but my parents are scientists, living in their labs, with my sister maybe becoming a doctor. So nobody in my family has a business or anything that I would want to work in."

She frowned, and he saw that, knowing she was already worried about him.

"I'm just letting some things roll around in my head," he

shared. "I have enough going on right now with rehab." He looked at her and said, "I know it's coffee time, but do you think there's any chance of a treat at the same time?"

"For you, always," she replied, "although I don't know that you need more sugar."

"I was wondering about ice cream."

She burst out laughing. "Ice cream's possible, definitely possible."

As they walked in the dining room, they saw no sign of Dennis, which was happening more and more, as he and the others were in the kitchen, always working on wedding things.

When he popped his head out and saw them, he stepped forward and noted, "You're early for dinner."

"We know," Nelly admitted, with a shrug. "Is there a chance of ice cream?"

"Ooh." Dennis's face lit up. "Absolutely." He disappeared and came back with two cones.

She looked at him and laughed. "I didn't even tell you what flavors."

"And I didn't ask 'cuz we didn't get our dairy delivery," he explained, "so these are the flavors." And he handed over two cones, one that had a bright pink something all through it and something else that had streaks of probably caramel.

She shook her head. "It doesn't matter what the flavors are. It will be delicious anyway."

"My thoughts exactly," Dennis replied. And, with that, he disappeared again into the kitchen.

She looked at Zander. "It's such a different air at the center right now." She had a big grin on her face. "I'm really loving it."

"Especially now that we got the you-know-what," he

whispered, looking around.

"Let's go out on the deck," she murmured. "And you're right. Now that we got that one locked down, I think this will make her wedding day so very special."

"It will, indeed," he agreed, "and I'm really proud to be invited."

"Was there any doubt about you coming?" she asked.

"No, but I felt like an interloper, until Aaron gave me a personal invite."

She frowned at him, and he explained about meeting him in person. "That's awesome. I knew everybody in Hathaway was invited, so I wasn't worried about it," she shared, with a smile. "So it's nice to know that you don't feel it's a problem now."

"No, not at all. And it is a pretty special time. As you said, a once-in-a-lifetime event."

"And just think, by the time the wedding gets here, you'll be walking around even more so than now."

"Does Dani have family, other than her father?"

"No. Aaron does. Dani doesn't, but she has close friends—many close friends. It'll be a big deal," she said, laughing.

AND ZANDER WAS happy for Dani. He really was. Yet all these wedding discussions were definitely making him think about his own future and what he wanted. As he saw the excitement build day after day, and sharing it with Nelly so much of the time, he realized just how special this whole thing was and how big a deal it seemed to be, especially for the women. "I guess you would like to have a big wedding too, wouldn't you?" he asked Nelly.

"Not necessarily. I would be happy to just go the courthouse and get married to somebody I love."

He nodded. "You don't want all this stuff?" he asked, as he waved a hand around, trying to encompass all the discussions and the secrets too.

"No, not at all. In this case it's appropriate because it's for Dani, and we have to keep so much of our plans secret," she added. "Yet I wouldn't want that. I would just want a simple ceremony."

He filed that away for later.

But then she looked at him and asked, "Why?"

And such an honest curiosity filled her tone that he realized she really had no idea. He shrugged. "Just something I was wondering about."

At that, somebody else interrupted them, for which Zander was grateful. But the thought crossing his mind was something that was hard to let go of. Same as he knew there was no way he would let go of her. They'd spent so much time together that she'd become a major part of his world. Yet he didn't think that she had any idea just how major. He frowned as he sat here.

When she looked over at him, catching him frowning, she offered, "Hey, if you want to leave, go for it."

He looked at her and realized that he'd more or less been ignoring her for the whole visit. He winced. "Sorry, I haven't been very good company."

"You're not here to be company for me," she noted. "If you want to go lie down, then lie down."

At that comment, he realized that she mistook his silence and his confusion and myriad thoughts for being tired. He looked at her, nodded gratefully, and added, "I think I will."

And, with that, he quickly made his escape.

Still, it didn't stop the thoughts in his mind that just seemed to circle and circle around in his head. *Was it too early to ask? Was it too fast? Did she care? Did she care enough? Did she not care at all?* Sighing heavily, he returned to his room, laid down, and, unbelievably, fell asleep.

Chapter 11

N ELLY NOTED THAT Zander acted differently now. Quieter, less happy. Several days later, when she saw him outside, sitting in his wheelchair, Nelly finally broached the subject. "You seem to be quite preoccupied recently."

He looked at her and smiled. "Yeah, that's one word for it."

She hesitated but asked, "Is it something I should know about?"

He shook his head. "No, not right now at least. I've just got something on my mind."

She nodded. "Sometimes when you have things on your mind … Well, I guess you'll get around to telling me whenever you are ready."

He nodded. "That's the way I was trying to look at it."

She nodded but found it hard to ignore the hurt. "And it's been really busy here lately, so I'm sure a lot has been going on that maybe hasn't made you happy."

He frowned at her. "Are patients complaining that I'm asking for donations?" he asked.

"No, no, not at all," she replied. "And we have talked to a few, wondering if all this wedding stuff was disturbing them. Yet they all seem to be really on board with it, but that doesn't mean that everybody is."

"Meaning me?" he asked. He shrugged. "You know I'm

totally okay with it."

"I was hoping so, but I'm not really sure what's going on then." When he didn't elaborate, she felt something inside her sinking. "But you're right," she added. "It's not anything I need to know about, at least at the moment." With a sigh she turned and looked around. "I need to go back to work."

He just nodded. He didn't say anything to change her trajectory.

Feeling out of sorts and not sure just what she was supposed to do about any of this, not knowing in what way any of this even affected her—except that she felt shut out, and maybe that was just the way life was sometimes. She didn't know. She didn't have enough experience in any of this personal relationship arena. He was doing so much better, but obviously something gnawed away at him.

Even Shane mentioned it to her a couple days later. "Any idea what's getting to him?" he asked Nelly.

"No," she admitted, shaking her head. "I've tried to talk to him a couple times, but he's not verbalizing it."

"That's not good," Shane noted, "because he should, and we don't want something building up inside him which could impact his progress, especially now that he's making some real strides."

"Yeah. If you find a way to make him open up, that would be great," she suggested. "I've tried. He basically is telling me that it's nothing I need to worry about."

"And obviously it is something we need to worry about if it's affecting him."

"I asked if the wedding stuff was getting to him, if maybe it was depressing him. He says no. ... I don't know, but everybody's got such a different reaction to it. Not everybody is happy, I presume."

"No, but most of them aren't feeling as if it's much of a big deal. It's a happy thing. As far as I can tell, everybody that I've spoken to is quite happy for Dani to finally get married. And the fact that Aaron is back again is also a big plus."

She nodded. "I've never seen Dani look this happy."

"Happy, yet stressed," Shane clarified, with a laugh.

"Now that's very true too," she admitted. "Still, the wedding's coming up in just a couple weeks now, so hopefully things can return to normal after that."

"And don't tell Dani that either," Shane noted. "Otherwise I'm afraid she'll take it as meaning that she's causing all this disruption."

"And she's not, not in any way," Nelly declared.

"Well, that wouldn't be quite true either," Shane murmured. "Still, it's not anything we want her to feel bad about."

"Right," she acknowledged. "That's the thing. It's busy enough and crazy enough around here that stuff will always be happening that we'll make allowances for. But the wedding is coming up fast, so …"

He nodded. "Very fast. I checked my calendar and realized it's just insane how fast it's coming now."

"And will the next couple to wed be you and Melissa afterward?" she teased.

"Maybe," he said, with a bright smile. "We plan to talk about it after Dani's wedding."

"I think there'll be a lot of those after-the-wedding discussions going on," she murmured.

"What about you?" he asked. "How are you and Zander getting along?"

"I thought we were doing fine, until this."

"And *this* doesn't have to be anything big," he reminded her.

"No, it doesn't, but it's such a weird feeling to get shut out like this," she acknowledged, "that I don't know. I'm, … I'm having some trouble dealing with it."

"Maybe you should tell him that too," Shane suggested. "You know it is something that you have to deal with because you're here. It's not as if you can get away from him and can give him time to get over it. You still have to discuss his nutrition and his needs and everything else."

"And I was avoiding that too because it just feels wrong to bring up anything right now."

"I wouldn't let it get too far down the road though," Shane warned her. "We can't afford to have him sick."

"He can't afford him to take any steps backward," she murmured, "but just because I tell him that, it doesn't mean that he's prepared to listen."

Shane frowned at that. "I could step in, but I was hoping not to have to."

"And I don't think you should," she admitted. "Honestly, I think it's far better if he has to get to the point where he can open up about whatever it is that's bothering him."

"And that would be great, as long as he does," Shane reminded her.

"Right, well, I'll give him another day or so."

And yet when another day went by, and there was still no improvement, she finally walked to his room and announced, "Hey, so we need to talk."

He looked at her. "What's up?"

"I'm not too sure what's going on with you, but everybody's starting to get worried."

He stared. "Have I been that out of it?" he asked slowly.

"Yep, you have been, and we all love you dearly, but we need to know if you're okay."

He smiled at her. "And you were elected to come see me?" he asked, but there was a teasing tone to his voice that just confused her even more.

"Well, somewhat." She frowned at him. "Apparently they think I might have a better chance of getting you to open up."

He chuckled at that. "And they're probably right."

"But I don't know that," she said. "I have to admit to feeling shut out these last few days."

At that, he stared at her in shock. "Oh, that's not what I wanted you to feel," he murmured. "And I'm sorry. I've been pondering something in my life, and I just didn't have an easy answer or a decision as to what to do about it."

"Interesting," she muttered, as she sat down. "Often though, when you have something that's bothering you, you discuss it with me. I can help find solutions for you hopefully. Even just sharing your worries can make you feel better. Yet this time you've made a point of isolating yourself."

"That's because it's—" He stopped and then winced. "It's private."

She took a slow, deep breath. "Okay, I get it. You're entitled to have something private here because it's not an easy place to be at all times. We all have some issues that we need to work out privately," she murmured. "But do you think you could come back to the land of the living a little more often while you're working on this problem? Or do I need to send Shane in to deal with this?"

Zander winced at that. "No, if I thought talking to Shane would have helped, I would have done it already."

"Okay." And again, not sure what she was supposed to

say with that information, she nodded. "Well, it would be great if you could put some of whatever is bothering you off to the side, so that other people aren't quite so worried about you."

"I can do that," he said.

She studied him for a moment and then asked, "Promise?"

"Absolutely," he said, with a bright smile. "And I really am sorry to worry you."

She nodded. "I get that. I really do, but when, … when you have people who care for you, and then you go silent, it makes people worry."

"And I guess I just didn't think anybody here would worry," he explained. "I'm, … I'm … I guess I haven't adapted to thinking that people cared."

"A lot of people care. If nothing else, this wedding deal should show you that."

"Sure, but it's Dani they care for."

"Absolutely, but that doesn't mean they don't care for anybody else." He just nodded, and she wasn't sure whether she was getting through to him or not. "I guess I would really like to be let in," she admitted. "But, if you feel like you can't let me in, then I will do my best to accept it and to let it go."

And, with that, she spun on her heels and left.

HOW ZANDER WAS supposed to handle this, he didn't know. Just because he didn't want to tell Nelly just yet what was on his mind didn't mean that she didn't deserve to know that he was okay. Frowning, he looked up when another head poked in. "Hey," he said to Shane. "Did she send you in next?"

"Does she need to?" he asked. "She's never really needed anybody to jump in before."

"And I would hope not now either," Zander replied, then winced. "Apparently I haven't been terribly communicative."

"No, you haven't, and I guess the issue is if it's something big that will slow your progress."

"It's not—Yeah, it is big," he confirmed, "but how am I supposed to talk to anybody about it, particularly her?"

"If you want to give me an idea," Shane began, "maybe I could find somebody here to talk to you about it. Did you talk to your therapist?"

"No." He shook his head. "I don't think that'll work somehow."

Shane looked at him, now with a wry smile. "Aah. We've all been through it."

Zander looked at him, startled. "Been through what?"

"Do you really think most of us don't know all this private consideration has been about your relationship with her?"

He winced at that. "That obvious, *huh?*"

"To us, but she hasn't a clue. I think inside she's worried that you are rejecting her. So the longer you take to open up and to talk to her about it, the harder it is for her to deal with it."

"I haven't opened up because I don't know what I want to do about it yet."

"In what way?"

"All this wedding stuff," he said, with a wave of his hand. "It gets a guy thinking."

At that, Shane laughed. "It so does. My partner and I have been discussing just that for quite a while," he admitted, with a smile. "And it's not the easiest thing to reconcile."

"No, it isn't, and I, … I don't know what I'm supposed to do about it."

"Why do you think that there's anything you need to do?" Shane asked, confused.

He stared at him. "Because I wanted … I'm thinking about asking her to marry me," he stated point-blank. "However, I'm hardly a good catch."

At that, Shane sank down at the end of his bed. "I've heard that time and time again here, and you are all wrong there," he murmured. "She spends all her time with you. Doesn't that tell you something? Doesn't that show you that she's interested in you?"

"That's part of the problem," he replied. "She and I are friends, good friends. But does she like me more than that? I feel as if I'm jumping the gun. Again it's all this wedding stuff that puts ideas in a guy's head."

Shane burst out laughing. "I get it. I really do get it. As for how she feels about you, you know the best answer is to just talk to her yourself."

"Yeah, but what if she doesn't feel the same? I just told you how I feel about not being whole and healthy, and yet I've come a long way. Still, I'm not there yet. I might never get there."

"You've come a very long way. You're up on your own legs. You're walking outside daily, even when rehab had you extremely tired. And you'll still get a bunch of those days when you leave here, no matter how it works out with Nelly down the road," Shane pointed out. "So it does seem as if you're holding on to a certain amount of worry over all this."

He looked at him and asked, "Wouldn't you be?"

"Yes, I absolutely would be. I absolutely was. However, when you know it's right, you know it's right."

"But when do you know it's right?" he asked curiously. "I've been sitting here, racking my brain about it, wondering how I'm supposed to know if it's right."

"Well, if you left Hathaway House tomorrow, and you didn't have her in your life anymore, how would you feel?"

"Bereft," he said instantly.

"That's a good start."

"But it's not me that I'm concerned about, it's her."

"She's never shown any interest in anybody else in this place except for you," Shane shared. "And I'm a firm believer that, when it's meant to be, it's meant to be. So you might want to just analyze a little more how the two of you interact and then get some better idea on her feelings for you. Personally I think you're on the right track. I don't know if she's quite ready for a commitment stage, but you won't know until you ask."

"And I could also just hold off and wait a little bit longer."

"You could, but considering it's affecting your ability to do your work here, and she seems more and more worried at your continued silence," Shane noted, "maybe you shouldn't."

"Is it affecting me?" He looked at him.

"You've been extremely unfocused. I guess that's a good word for it. I was coming in to talk to you about it right now, but I saw her leaving, and she didn't look as if she was doing very well. So the question is, do I need to separate the two of you, so that you aren't out of focus all the time and so that she isn't having a negative impact on you?"

"That would *not* be a good idea," Zander declared bluntly. "And I get that, from your perspective, it probably seems as if she's the reason I'm not doing all that well, but you would be wrong."

"Maybe, but you need to prove that to me. I'm not really seeing it yet."

He stared at Shane. "How does anybody prove that?" he asked, bewildered.

"Show me that she's not the reason your focus is scattered, for a start," Shane replied. "And, when we have our session tomorrow, you show up 100 percent and not just at 50."

He stared at him. "You're saying that I didn't even realize that I was slacking?"

"Well, you are slacking," Shane said bluntly. "And now, if we've got that out of the way, I suggest you deal with whatever it is that's bothering you as much as you can right now. Then tomorrow, when you're ready, you get down there, and we knock your workout outta the park."

"Got it," he muttered.

Long after Shane left, Zander worried on it. The last thing he wanted was for Shane to keep her away from him, thinking that she was having a negative effect on him. He quickly texted Shane. **Don't move her.**

Shane replied, **We'll see tomorrow.**

Great, Zander muttered to himself. Now there's no end to the stress that he was putting on himself. If he hadn't texted Shane, maybe it wouldn't have been quite so stressful. He shook his head at it all. He hadn't come here for this, and yet, in the back of his mind, he wondered, seriously wondered, if there was any chance of finding somebody in here to help him. At that, he picked up his phone and contacted Xavier.

When his friend answered the phone, they talked about aimless stuff for the first little bit, and then Zander finally got to the heart of the matter. "I've got a problem."

"Yeah, usually, when you call, you do," he replied, with a laugh.

He explained about Shane's ultimatum.

"Ouch, that's not like you."

"I know it isn't, and I did get off track. I didn't realize how badly people were affected by it because I got myself into another bit of a spot."

"Tell me more. You know you can always talk to me about anything."

"Yeah, but it's not something that I ever really expected to talk to anybody about," he murmured.

At that, his friend laughed. "Okay, now I'm really curious. So what's going on?"

He hesitated and then admitted, "It's Nelly."

"What about her?" And there was only curiosity in his friend's voice.

"I think all this wedding stuff is getting to me," he added quickly. "And it's a stupid idea."

"Yeah, well, we've had a lot of stupid ideas, and they didn't rack you up sideways and stop you from sleeping and get you in trouble with your PT therapist," Xavier shared. "So what's going on?"

"I really love her," he murmured. "And I was wondering about asking her to marry me. And I'm putting all that down to all this wedding stuff going on here."

At that, Xavier whistled. "Dude, nobody would be happier than me if she said yes."

"I know I can talk to you about anything. I just don't know that you understand the problem I'm going through right now."

Xavier snorted. "Seriously? You don't know if I'll understand? Remember that I just went through this."

"Sure, but you did get through it," Zander pointed out. "I'm not *through* anything. I'm caught up in the crazy middle part that just makes no sense."

"And I was there too," he reminded his friend. "And I can tell you that, as soon as you get to the other side, everything is so much more worthwhile."

"And what if she says no?"

There was silence on the other end. "Do you think she'll say no?"

"No. I don't know. I have no idea how she feels about me," he shared.

"That's not true," Xavier argued. "You wouldn't even be contemplating what you're talking to me about if you didn't think that she returned your feelings."

"Sure, but I also don't know that she returns them in the same way."

"Now that I can see," he acknowledged, "but still that's fear and doubt speaking."

"Sure, none of this is easy. How am I supposed to expect her to want to spend a life with me, when I'm still such a mess?"

"Yeah, I had the same arguments with my partner," he replied. "And I can tell you that she got quite angry with me for even thinking along that route. Yet it's automatic for us to do such a thing because we don't know how any of this will play out. And then she asked me that, if she had an accident, would I bail on her?"

"Of course not," Zander declared. "And why the heck would we bail when we're the ones who are the best to guide them through it? We've already been there."

"Exactly," Xavier noted, "and that was her point. If I wasn't the guy who would be there for her, then she wasn't interested. And, when I tried to reassure her that I was, her point was *Then why would you insult me by assuming that I wasn't the person who cared about the trouble you're in now?*"

"Oh." Zander sat back in his chair. "I didn't think of that."

"No, I didn't either," Xavier said. "And you can bet that was quite an eye-opener."

"You're quite right," he murmured. "I absolutely would be the one to stick around and to help her out. Obviously I wouldn't want to wish this on anybody, but, considering that we do have the skills to deal with this stuff, that would not be a hardship for us."

"No, it wouldn't, but it would be a hardship for them," he stated. "So I would think seriously about what it is you want out of life, what it is you want out of this new life that you are working on right now, and then how you're still better off to know, one way or the other, how Nelly feels about all this. Maybe instead of popping the question, have a discussion with her first. See if marriage is even on the page for her."

"Well, it is. We've already had some discussions about that in a general sense," he replied cautiously.

"So then I see this as just more a case of nerves for you."

"Sure," he agreed, with a laugh. "It's always about nerves."

"And, of course, the last woman you asked to marry you said no."

"Exactly, and I really don't want a repeat."

"Right. That was a very long time ago, and I think you were also three-quarters drunk," Xavier noted.

"I had to get drunk to get the nerve up," Zander replied.

"And then you wonder why she said no?" Xavier asked, then laughed.

"I know, but, hey, at least I tried."

"And that's the lesson for you right now, is at least you tried back then. And you care so much more right now that you don't need to get drunk first," Xavier declared. "I'll be cheering you on from the sidelines."

And, with that, his best friend disconnected.

Chapter 12

WHEN NELLY CAUGHT sight of Shane a couple days later in the hallway, she asked in a quiet voice, "Any improvement?"

He nodded. "Still didn't get a clear answer as to what's going on," he replied, his voice equally quiet. "Did you?"

She shook her head. "No, I'm just trying to support him as best I can."

"And honestly, I think that's probably wise," he murmured.

She and Shane were walking back to her office, when she looked up to see Zander coming down the hallway, toward the dining room. She smiled and asked, "Ready for lunch?"

"Absolutely," Zander replied. He looked over at Shane. "I did better today, right?"

"You did, and I'm glad to see it." And, with that, he waved and turned and left them alone.

"Shane give you a talking to or something?" she asked curiously.

He nodded. "Apparently I was slacking."

"Oops, Shane doesn't like slackers," she said, with a chuckle.

"Right, and he was right to call me out on it," Zander admitted.

She just looked at him, but he didn't say anything more.

She found that incredibly hard to take, still being shut out of Zander's life.

As they walked into the dining room, he asked, "How about we take our food to the garden area?"

He seemed more personable, acting like he used to, something she hadn't seen out of him in a few days. She nodded and smiled at him. "Sure. It would be like a picnic."

"Did I hear the word *picnic*?" Dennis asked, standing behind the buffet line. He looked down at the food under the glass and waved a hand. "You can get something from here, or you can give me a few minutes, and I can do you up a real picnic basket."

"Oh, that would be lovely," she said warmly, "but I know you're busy."

"I am, but that's all right. I do like it when picnics happen here too."

At that, she looked over at Zander. "You okay to wait?"

"I'm okay to wait. I didn't know picnics were an option."

"I'm not sure I did either," she said, with a laugh. "Are you just wanting to get outside for some fresh air? Or to avoid too much wedding planning?"

"Not avoiding the wedding planning," he replied. "I can't believe that it's in ten days."

"I know. It'll be quite the event."

He added, "I just want to get outside a bit, and maybe visit with you without everybody watching."

She nodded. "Sounds good to me."

Dennis handed them a picnic basket about ten minutes later.

She took it and muttered, "It's pretty heavy. Dennis, what did you put in here?"

"It's a surprise," he said. "Just bring it back when you're done."

And, with that, Zander took over the picnic basket, putting it in his lap, as he was in his wheelchair. Then they took the elevator down and ran into Stan, who smiled at the picnic basket.

"That's a really good idea," he noted. "We have lots of pastures and pathways and all kinds of stuff outside to enjoy, besides all the animals. I know Bella was making benches for people to sit on around the area too. I think picnic tables will be next."

"Sounds like a great idea," Nelly said.

And, with that, they headed out, bypassed the pool and took a path down to one of the big walkways that ran past the pastures.

"Where would you like to go?" she asked Zander.

"Just keep walking, and we'll find a place that's just right," he replied.

And, with that, she walked casually down the path, pushing his chair, tilting her face up to the sun.

Zander murmured, "It's a beautiful day."

"It absolutely is," she agreed, with a big smile.

"Every day in Texas is a beautiful day in some ways."

"In some ways, yes. However, in some ways, no," she clarified. "It seems as if there's always more going on than you expect." He didn't say anything to that. She looked over at him. "Did you solve whatever problem was bothering you?"

"I did, indeed," he confirmed, and his smile was so gentle that she wasn't exactly sure what to make of it.

When he pulled up in a grassy spot, off to the side, he said, "This looks good." He slowly stepped out of the wheelchair and sat down on the grass. She sat down beside him. As they opened up the basket, he realized a big blanket was inside, just perfect for the picnic. "Oops, I guess we should have known about that first, *huh?*"

"We know now," she declared, as she spread it out, and they put the food on it. "With all your walking exercises and the weight training too, how are the legs doing?" she asked.

"All of me is doing much better," he shared, "but the workouts are pretty strenuous. So I wasn't sure how far I would get."

"Ah." She nodded. "So you wanted to do this anyway this morning, even after your rehab workout."

"Yep," he said, with that same smile.

As they opened the basket to see what else was in there, he pulled out wine glasses and a bottle of wine. "Wow, if I'd realized we were allowed alcohol …"

She chuckled. "I'm not sure what to say about this either."

He opened the wine and poured two glasses, and she tilted hers up, and they clinked them together.

"To us," he said.

"Absolutely," she murmured and clinked her glass against his. She took a sip and smiled. "Oh, this is lovely." She looked down at the label. "I'll have to remember it."

"We can ask Dennis too. I didn't even know that alcohol was around the place."

"There's been alcohol for various events," she shared, "just not much of it. None of the patients are allowed it individually."

He nodded. "And I certainly haven't been offered any recently," he admitted, with a laugh, "so that makes sense."

With that, they put their glasses down and dug into the

food that Dennis had selected. Opening containers, they found meat pies, green salads, a potato salad, and a meat and cheese platter.

"I think that was supposed to go with the wine," Zander noted. "Oops."

She chuckled. "Hey, it's not as if we got a menu presented to us."

"Nope, we didn't," he agreed, as he picked up a cube of cheese and popped it in his mouth. "It's lovely though."

And they sat here, quite content, and ate their lunch. He kept looking at her. When she would look up, he would look away. She frowned at that. When she was done eating, she picked up a cube of cheese, studied it for a moment, and then asked, "So what's on your mind?"

"What makes you think something's on my mind?"

"Oh, I'm not a fool," she said.

"No, you're not. You're beautiful, intelligent, and an absolutely lovely person."

She stared at him and then chuckled. "I don't know what brought that on, but you need to tell me so that I can do whatever again."

He laughed. "I don't need to tell you anything. You … it's just been such an eye-opener to see everybody here. I didn't really realize how much I was being affected by all of it, until all this wedding stuff got closer and closer."

"Ten days," she stated, "and then it will calm down. I promise."

"And I'm okay with that," he replied. "Don't get me wrong. I'm so thrilled for this to be going on. It just brought up a lot of memories for me as to what I wanted out of life, where I thought I would be by now."

"Ah"—she nodded—"those kinds of thoughts can be tough."

"They can be very tough," he agreed, with a nod. "Also you don't really think about it so much until everybody around you is making plans. I know Shane mentioned how he and his partner will discuss their own marriage, once Dani's wedding is over."

"Exactly." Nelly nodded. "I've heard that from multiple people at this point."

"So I wasn't trying to avoid … discussing this," he began. "I just didn't know where my own thoughts were."

"I'm sorry that you didn't feel as if you could tell me that though," she shared. "I would have understood."

"Of course you would," he noted. "You guys specialize in understanding at levels that I've never seen before. And it's not a criticism in any way. It was just something that I had to work out for myself."

"And I get that too," she murmured. "I hope you got it figured out now."

"Oh, I think I did," he shared. "What I didn't really know, and why I couldn't really involve you in all of my thought processes, was how you felt."

She stared at him. "How I felt? Are you saying, *past tense?*"

He looked at her, shook his head. "When I was thinking about it, it was past tense," he explained. "But I'm certainly not trying to keep that conversation in the past tense."

She looked confused for a moment and then realized it didn't matter. "What you're really asking is how I feel about you, is that it?"

He looked at her and then nodded. "Yes, essentially yes."

"I think that should be obvious by now. I wouldn't be here with you if I didn't care."

"But how much do you care?" he asked, with a sigh.

"That's what I've been trying to sort through in my head."

She opened her mouth, thinking that she had an answer and then closed it again.

"See? I've been doing a lot of that myself," he admitted. He picked up a cube of cheese, held it out to her, and when she opened her mouth, he popped it in, with a laugh. "I would like to think that we're on the same page. I'm just not sure that we're both on the *same*-same page."

"I would love to get to know you more and to spend the time that we have together exploring a relationship," she declared. "Yet I don't want you to feel rushed. Plus, I really don't want you to focus on a relationship at the cost of your own health."

"Ah, and there comes the real practical aspects again, right?" And again she looked a little confused. He smiled. "You see? You guys are all so concerned about us patients that we never really understand where the relationship is. I get that things have changed, and you're allowed to have relationships now," he noted. "And thank heavens for that, but it also doesn't necessarily help me sort through my confusion."

"No, I guess maybe not," she replied cautiously and then frowned. "I thought we were pretty clear on both of us."

"We were," he said, but then with a wave of his hand he nullified that by saying, "until all this wedding stuff."

"I don't get how this wedding stuff changes anything."

"For you, maybe not," he acknowledged, "but, for me, it was a bit more of an eye-opener than I had expected to be questioning myself about."

"Meaning that you don't think you're ready for a relationship, and you're afraid I'm pushing it?"

"Oh my goodness, no." He stared at her. "That's not

what I mean."

Then she frowned. "Okay, so now I'm really confused," she murmured. "And I'm glad to hear that that's not what you meant, but you're in a roundabout way saying nothing, when I would really prefer that you just came right out and said it."

He stared at her and smiled, the corner of his lips twitching. "If you want me to, yes, I can do that. It just might not be terribly classy."

"*Classy* isn't really the issue here," she stated, her back stiffening. "I really think you should just make this as clear as mud. Because I don't want there to be any misunderstandings."

ZANDER COULD ALREADY tell from the way she was talking that there was a big misunderstanding.

He picked up her hand, placed it against his lips, kissing her fingers. "Fine, as bluntly as I can, will you please marry me?"

She gasped in shock, clapping her free hand to her lips.

He grinned. "I'm hoping that that's a yes, but I'm really not sure. So you'll have to make it as equally clear to me," he said, trying for a light-hearted approach. Yet inside he felt everything tightening, as he waited for her answer.

Sure, he hadn't really asked the last person to marry him with any care because, well, he'd been drunk at the time. Still, it'd seemed like a good idea. It was one of the reasons he wasn't much of a drinker anymore because, when it happened, he tended to do foolish things like that. He found he'd needed the alcohol to work up the courage back then.

That woman thankfully had been just as drunk and had laughed him out of the bar. Still, Zander hadn't forgotten the sting of being rejected, even under those somewhat forgettable circumstances.

Nelly started to giggle. "The last thing I expected was a marriage proposal. I was so focused on making sure that you were really clear about what you were trying to say. Yet I was worried that maybe I'd done something wrong or that you were trying to break up with me or even warning me that you weren't quite ready for as much as I was ready for."

"And yet in some ways," he explained, "it seemed like the natural next step. Having all these wedding discussions was also something that played on my mind too."

"At the same time though, I never expected for you to ask me."

"Why?"

"Because of the way you've mentioned things, as if you needed more time."

"I need more time, yes," he agreed. "I need more time here. I need more time to build up, to get stronger than I was before. But I don't need more time to understand what I want to do with my life, which is, spending it with you. Are you saying yes?" he asked. He stroked her bottom lip. "Because I'm hearing no."

"If you're hearing no," she stated firmly, "that's your fear. You're afraid I'll say no even though I've said yes."

"Have you said yes?"

"Yes, I'm saying yes," she declared, a big smile on her face.

"Maybe I would like a little bit more of a reaction than that," he muttered, staring at her. "Maybe if you would scream in joy or throw your arms around me or do something to make me feel like you actually believe that this is a good thing."

At that, she slipped over closer. "I think it's a wonderful thing," she whispered warmly. "I was just surprised that you actually asked me, when I wasn't even thinking that you were close to asking me," she explained. "So it's only my shock as to why I'm still sitting here, stunned." As she slid her arms up his chest to wrap around his neck, she added, "But the answer is absolutely yes, as in yes, please. And if you want to wait until you're out of here to marry, that's fine. However, if you don't want to wait, I'm totally okay to get married in the next couple weeks."

He stared at her in shock. "Seriously?"

"Absolutely," she declared. "I've learned one thing about Dani's situation, and I don't need or want a big wedding," she shared. "Just like Dani didn't need it, but we all understand why it's necessary this time to have it this way. I would like to get married with a small group of people and preferably sooner than later."

"Are you sure you don't want me fully recovered from here?"

She shook her head. "No, I don't. I want to marry you now, or at least after Dani's wedding. You'll almost be out of here by then anyway," she noted. "But considering that I don't want to wait, I'm hoping that you don't want to wait either, so we have no reason to wait, right?"

He smiled, pulled her closer, and whispered, "You're saying everything my heart wants to hear, and again, like you, I guess I'm just in shock."

"Absolutely," she said, with a chuckle. "And you won't change your mind, right? When the wedding things are over, you won't feel as if you were rushed into it?"

He smiled at her and shook his head. "Never, and that's why I've been so confused these last few days. And I couldn't talk to you about it because it was you I was confused over."

"Oh." She frowned. "So you weren't undecided as to whether you wanted to marry me or not?"

"No," he stated, placing a finger over her lips. "Only concerned as to whether *you* wanted to marry *me*. And I was afraid that you didn't care enough."

"Oh, I care enough," she declared, "and it's been so hard to stay detached and to let you do your own thing, when I just wanted to spend time with you and wanted to let you know that whatever you needed to share with me was okay. And I wouldn't judge you for it, yet I would be more than happy to help you work your way through this problem—or any others."

"And you just have," he said and started to chuckle.

She looked at him and grinned herself. "We do weave a tangled web, don't we?" she asked, giggling.

"Indeed," he murmured. He pulled her tightly against him and held her close. "And thank you, for making it mud clear."

She burst out laughing. "I suggest that the next time either one of us has something that we need to sort through, that we do it together. And fast, as in immediately. It might help ease some of this confusion—and hurt feelings."

"Oh, I agree. Absolutely." He pulled her even tighter and whispered, "How about a kiss to seal the deal?"

She tilted her head up and whispered back, "Yes, please."

And he lowered his head and kissed her with all the longing that he had in his heart. Nelly's instant response made him feel whole and happy for the first time in a very long time.

T HE BRIGHT SUNSHINE broke through the clouds and bathed Hathaway House in a warm glow. Standing just inside on the bottom floor, ready to walk out to the makeshift aisle and altar, Dani looked up at her father. "Are you ready for this?" she asked nervously.

He looked down at her, patted her tenderly, and replied, "I've been waiting a lifetime for this."

She smiled, feeling her heart swell and her nerves calm. "So have I," she muttered. "So have I."

And as they walked out through the double doors, she heard the music and recognized Lance on the piano, now outside. He'd come back to play live music for her special day. Up ahead Aaron stood proud and tall, his brother Levi standing by him as his best man. She smiled up at Levi, the best friend she could have ever had. And now to know that she was marrying Aaron, the man she loved after all this time just made her heart swell with joy.

Plus, she had witnesses all around her to share her joy—friends, family, patients, former patients, and friends and family of patients. It seemed like Hathaway had opened its doors and out had tumbled hundreds and hundreds of people, maybe even thousands. She had no idea even who all was here, but she could see the staff standing up close to the altar. They'd put flowers on both sides of the designated seating areas, and animals galore dotted the place, as everybody in the vet clinic was out, animals leashed at their sides, to see a piece of the action as well. Three-legged Helga walked ahead of Dani, carrying the rings in a bag secured around her collar.

Dani smiled, tears in her eyes, as she whispered, "Look at this, just look at this."

The Major smiled and chuckled. "I think they had more fun planning this than you did."

She smiled up at him and nodded. "They wouldn't let me have a small wedding."

"Nope, this is very much what you needed."

"No." She shook her head. "I just needed Aaron."

He nodded. "But it's not just you anymore, sweetheart. It's Hathaway House too. You created this, and you made this happen, and everybody here wants to let you know just how they feel about you and this special place."

With more tears collecting in her eyes, she walked down until they were right in front of Aaron. And then her father handed her off to her husband-to-be, and she stood up at the altar to make her vows. When the vows were done, and, after they kissed, Aaron lifted his head. She smiled up at him through the din of the crowd cheering around them, and she whispered, "Finally."

He chuckled, pulled her close, and whispered, "Finally, indeed. It's been a long time coming."

She nodded. "You're not kidding."

And she turned to face the crowd, waving, that's when she saw a beautiful dappled gray mare coming down the pathway toward her, Stan walking calmly at her side.

"Oh my gosh." Dani gasped as she studied the mare. So beautiful. So familiar. And then it hit her. *Sunshine.* "No."

She shook her head. "No, it can't be."

"Oh, I think it probably can be," Stan countered, as he led the beautiful horse toward her.

She took one look at him, then the mare, picked up her wedding dress so that she could run, and raced toward Sunshine, throwing her arms up and around the mare's beautiful neck. The horse, instead of backing away, leaned in and nickered gently against her neck. Sunshine remembered Dani. Tears blurred her vision as her throat was choked with emotions. Letting Sunshine go all those years ago had been the hardest of decisions. To think that she had Sunshine back …

Dani could barely see the crowd around them, her tears nonstop in her eyes.

Stan explained to the audience that this horse was one that Dani had given up after many, many years as a family pet in order to start Hathaway House. And it was only fair that, as Dani had suffered this loss and had given something from that loss to everybody else, that something good should come from it as well. And they had worked hard to find the mare and to give Dani back a piece of her soul and a part of her heart that she had given up, just as she continued to give up her heart and soul every day for the last many years for every patient at Hathaway House.

As Dani turned and looked at Stan, with tears rolling down her face, she whispered, "Thank you," and the rest of the wedding party started to cheer.

This ends the series of heartwarming stories from Hathaway House.

The Haven: Timber (Book #1)

Welcome to an exciting new series by USA Today Bestselling Author Dale Mayer. The Haven is a sanctuary for both animals and humans in need. Step into Timber's world, a beloved character from the popular K9 Files series, where cherished animals receive the care they deserve, and friends find a helping hand.

This series blends romance, suspense, and has a deep focus on character development. Follow these men as they stand at the crossroads of a new life, using their time at The Haven to discover their paths and the companions who will join them.

Find Book 1 here!

To find out more visit Dale Mayer's website.

https://geni.us/DMSTHTimber

Excerpt from Timber
Chapter 1

TIMBER WOODLAND STRAIGHTENED from his project, wincing at the jolt of pain, and reached for the old T-shirt hanging from a nail on the wood post beside him. He used it to stop the sweat from running down his face, then took a moment to wipe his hands before rehanging the rag. Even in shorts and a tank top, he couldn't stop the sweat from forming. It was New Mexico in the summertime, after all.

Stretching his arms out first, he next moved around a few steps to loosen up the joints in his legs. It was one thing to work outdoors all day long. It was another thing to work outdoors all day long and to feel every muscle screaming at him at the end of the day—something he wanted to avoid as much as he could. Yet still he pushed himself to the very limit, testing where that line was daily.

He sighed. His life had been broken in two. Before the accident and after.

Before, he had always been a fitness fanatic, easily making it into the Navy SEALs, plus adding field medic to his skills.

And afterward? Well, to be honest, his prosthetic tried to slow him down. He shook his head at that. He had too much to do, and the dream of the Haven, an animal rescue and rehabilitation center, drove him.

He smiled as he felt a sense of accomplishment, a sense of a job well-done. It was hard to explain if you'd never really experienced it, but, to Timber, life was meant to be lived. That meant to have a body that was well used too. It's just that *used* seemed to be a second cousin to *abused*, something Timber constantly kept an eye on.

It had taken a long time to get into the physical shape he was in, and the last thing he wanted was to lose it over carelessness now. Of course it could happen in a heartbeat if he injured himself or if he overdid it on a regular basis. It was hard not to. He was alone and doing everything himself. Therefore, he was overdoing it himself daily.

Yet he had healed enough to finally walk freely on his prosthetic, and doing construction work for Badger over the past many months had been better than rehab. Plus the added design work that he did for Kat had helped Timber and Kat to further refine his prosthetic. So each kind of work had also been a form of mental and physical therapy, but a program that he was sure his former physiotherapist wouldn't have expected or would even have allowed.

Regardless, moving heavy construction materials, swinging a hammer, and climbing timber frames on construction jobs, as Badger's crew worked to build houses for those in need, had helped Timber in so many ways, even after he had left them to put down roots here.

And now his body moved with a freedom he rejoiced in. He just needed to remember that tomorrow would be a whole different story if he didn't look after today.

How prophetic. If everybody would learn that simple lesson, things would be a whole lot easier. But people didn't seem to learn easily, and he was no exception.

He stepped back, took a look at his work, and nodded. It was coming along. It was slow, and that was fine, since it was his and his alone. It was a dream come true, even if it was in a very dilapidated state right now. He was perfectly capable of fixing it. It would just take time, energy, and money. Doing it fast would be great, but he was just fine to settle on doing it well.

He took several more steps, kicking out his legs, readjusting his prosthetic ever so slightly, making note of where it was hurting and wondering whether he was doing something wrong or should really bring it up with Kat.

As a prosthetics designer and manufacturer, she'd been instrumental in getting his mobility to this point, and he appreciated it. Finding her and Badger had truly been a blessing in disguise, and, through that construction work for them, Timber had concluded that *this* was what he needed to do.

One of Timber's dogs, Kojack, a Heinz 57 mix but with a bit of Lab in him, raced over to Timber, then slightly detoured to chase a squirrel that had been keeping him company all morning. Timber quickly corrected the dog's behavior, as the squirrel was just as welcome here as the dogs were. Kojack had been badly abused in his early years and now had almost no hair on most of his body, but he had a heck of a good sniffer and was a great watchdog.

Even if he wasn't, Timber would have taken him in a heartbeat because Kojack needed a home, and that was what Timber was all about. If an animal needed something that Timber could provide, he was there for them.

He reached down to scrub the back of Kojack's head. He barked and rubbed against Timber's exposed legs. The animals didn't care about Timber's prosthetic, injuries, or scars. They just cared about the fact that Timber was here for them. They now existed in a world full of joy, contentment, peace, and even fun because they were out here playing on a regular basis. For Timber it was work, but, since his toil was for the dogs and for the future animals too, well, it was everything.

He laughed when Kojack raced over as Philly, a brown Malinois, got up and slowly moved toward him. Philly was an older shepherd, probably a K9 dog at one point in time, but her training had been a long time ago. Now she was much more concerned about where her next meal was than where the next villain of the story was. Timber was fine with that. She was a sweetheart, and she moved about gingerly, probably just as sore and stiff as he was some days.

He bent to stroke her forehead. "Hey, girl. How are you doing?"

While cuddling her, he surveyed his property. He had over sixty acres now and was hoping to get more from the owner of the ranch next door. It was land the current owner wasn't using, land that even now the family was trying to break up and to sell off in bits and pieces, just so they could get the money for other things. And the old man, Andy Killerman, was holding off as much as he could.

Timber didn't want to be part of the breakup of the Killerman family land, but, if any of that land was available to come his way, he was more than happy to negotiate. So far, Andy had been more than reasonable, and Timber appreciated that; but he also understood that the rest of the Killerman family didn't see it the same way. If Andy bent to their wills, they would want Andy to make a deal on the land. Timber knew that the prices would likely go way up too, and that was something he didn't want.

When it came to Andy though, it was anybody's bet. He was a rancher through and through, and he knew what a deal was. He knew what the value of his property was. So, as much as he had been happy to let Timber have some acreage, Andy was still holding off on the rest of the property, and that was fine.

Sixty acres was more than enough for Timber to deal with right now. He'd hoped for ten, twenty, and it had turned into thirty, then doubled from there. In truth, sixty acres had been a godsend for him, particularly when it came with a watering hole on the side, which meant that chances were good that he would have a decent water supply.

He could always put in more wells, and he already had one for the main cabin, his house, but one never had quite enough water, particularly in this New Mexico area. Once again he grabbed the rag, wiped off his face, then reached for his water bottle and took a big slug. He would love a cold beer right now, but not until the day was done. Only then would he consider it. Right now, there was work, … hell, there was always work.

Feeling an odd sensation coil up his back, he shifted ever so slightly to see what his internal antenna had caught, whatever the hell that meant anymore. When he had been a US Navy SEAL, his instincts had been his saving grace many a time, and he had certainly kept them cultivated and fine-tuned, but what the hell that meant in his current life, he had no clue. His life was completely different than he'd expected it to be. That's what happened when you got injured on the job, particularly to the level of the injury that Timber had sustained.

He looked around once more, the warning tingles gone. So was the animal that didn't want to approach. At least not yet. If hurting enough, the animal would return to get some help from Timber, as Timber had done for himself. He now smiled down at his steel blue prosthetic. His prosthetic was top-notch, and that was due to Kat. He'd also helped her to build some jigs to make some of the processing of these individual one-off pieces a little easier for her, and, as a thank-you—and her hope for continued assistance from Timber—she had been helping him build these prosthetics for his own leg. This one was doing pretty well, and he was really happy with the way it had worked out. Still smiling, he quickly texted Kat just to share that. She deserved to know that things were going well.

She responded, **Good. I would like to see it in a couple weeks, just to assess how it's holding up against the hard work.**

He laughed at that, since he'd worked damn hard when he was on Badger's crew, but this personal work of Timber's was a little different, and he knew that she understood that. He sent her a thumbs-up, popped his phone back into his pocket, and reached for his hammer again. He'd replaced the boards on the outside deck already and the support beams for the roof that would go on top. There had been an old awning, but time and weather had completely destroyed that to the point where he'd ripped it down and reframed it for a permanent roof atop the deck.

Not everybody would see that as a priority, but he had certainly identified this project as something he could do fairly quickly and would have a big impact on his lifestyle. He was an outdoor boy through and through, and having a deck, particularly when the weather was up and down, would be a big boon. Not to mention that the animals thoroughly appreciated it. He laughed, reached down, and scratched

Philly on the back of her neck. She just looked up at him, her tail wagging. "I know, girl. We're almost done for the day."

Kojack barked at him, and Timber picked up the ball on the ground nearby and tossed it for him. He knew it was a game that would never end because Kojack had a ball fixation that just didn't quit. And that was okay, as long as he understood that, when work had to be done, that took priority. The dog didn't understand in the least, of course, but that was all right too.

Timber laughed as Kojack dropped the ball at his side. Timber threw it a few more times while he had a few more sips of water. Then he returned to measuring and ensuring everything was level and plumb. With the new post up, his next plan was to get the ridge framework secured to each post and also to the existing roof on this main cabin. Then he would put up the rafters, followed by the plywood, some waterproofing, and, before long, it would be a permanent roof.

He had shingles nearby, and, as long as the weather held, he should be okay to finish off the roof in the next day or so. He needed to go into town and get more supplies, but he was holding off as long as he could. Town was just that, *town*, and that meant people, so not his favorite thing to do, but he also had to take Lucy in for her checkup.

He looked over where she was, in the basket beside her brother. Lucy and Bingo, both King Charles spaniels, had been rescues that came his way within days of his moving here. He just smiled as Lucy looked up, batted her eyelids at him, and stretched out. She was now missing a leg and was still adjusting to life without that extra support. She would take any affection and love coming her way, particularly if it meant she got to be carried around, something she was way too accustomed to.

The previous owners hadn't taken her to be checked until she'd somehow gotten an ugly infection that would cost her a leg. They wanted her put down instead, but Timber happened to be there, picking up Philly from her checkup, when he'd heard about Lucy. He'd talked to the vet Tiffany, a young woman he couldn't help but admire, and Lucy's surgery had been done, with Timber taking care of her ever since.

The owners, hearing about it, had given him Bingo, as the two siblings were bonded. Lucy was such a sweetheart, but she was currently one of the biggest financial draws on the place. She wasn't exactly a contributing member of the property, and that was all right too, as far as Timber was concerned. Not everybody had to pull their weight. Some of them got away with doing absolutely nothing but eating and sleeping and looking for love.

Her brother Bingo had somewhat adopted her lifestyle, sticking close by her side, as if understanding that her life had changed in ways that nobody had expected. Timber knew firsthand how that felt. He understood that everybody needed support at times, and right now Lucy was at the top of the list.

Yet surely she must sometimes think that all this was way too much. She'd been hard-pressed to even try to get up and walk, but something about being outdoors with the other animals had urged her to take a few steps, then a few more and a few more. Her balance was still terrible, and she fell several times, but she was improving every day. As long as Timber could get her to keep getting up and getting out a bit, life would be that much easier on her.

He walked over, bent down, gave her a quick cuddle, then said hello to Bingo, who stretched out a paw right beside him. Timber had to laugh. "The two of you are the laziest dogs I've ever seen."

Lucy gave half a bark, high-pitched but excited. Any time he talked to her, she always had the same reaction, as if she was absolutely thrilled that somebody was taking a moment to say hi. He always wondered how animals ended up with some of the people that they did. He didn't blame the previous owners; Lucy had come down with a serious infection, and most pet owners would have chosen to put her down. Yet Timber saw the value in her and knew she deserved a chance to live, but that didn't mean everybody would.

He straightened up once more, then looked back and announced, "Come on. Let's get those timbers up, as long as we've got the crossbeams in place. These upright ones won't hold against the wind." And, with that, he got back to work, but his instincts once again had him looking around a few minutes later, a weird feeling prodding him. Frowning at not seeing anything still, he headed back to get more work done. Yet he was always aware of that weird sense of something off, something wrong.

Finally, with the crossbeams up and everything tightened down, he looked over at Kojack. "You haven't picked up on anything, have you, buddy?"

Kojack just wagged his tail.

That meant their earlier visitor wasn't human. Kojack had a very strong sense of anything human, with good reason, but that also meant it was an animal, probably feral. And Timber had just enough wounded animals around the place that, if this new visitor was a predator, that would make sense. Yet often Timber found that, even if a predator, it could still need help. He preferred to think that some automatic distribution system sent the animals in need to find their way to him, and then he would do what he could. His time as a field medic in the military held him in good stead for most things, on two legs or four.

When it was something more serious, he had a great relationship with the veterinarians in town, mostly because he kept bringing them so much business. But they also gave him a hell of a deal, and, more often than not, he ended up getting their services and their supplies for cost. He couldn't ask them for more than that because everybody had bills to pay.

When he was finally done for the day, he stopped, grabbed his water bottle, then slowly opened his sixth-sense gaze, focusing on his peripheral vision, trying to determine just what he had been sensing. Catching the barest hint of movement off to the side, he froze and saw a deer, staring back at him. Even from here, he felt the waves of pain coming off her. Ordering the dogs to sit, he slowly backed up in her direction, trying not to scare her, not at all sure just what he was looking at or why she was here. He didn't know whether she was injured or something else was going on. He hoped it wasn't serious.

As he got closer, he shifted just enough to take another look at her. She was standing on four legs, but holding her weight off the front. She stood between multiple branches, so it was much harder for him to get a clear impression of her, but, when he did see it, his gaze sharpened as he assessed the situation, and then the anger hit—and hit hard.

An arrow was sticking out of her shoulder, and it seemed to have been there for way-the-hell too long.

Knowing that he would now be tasked with the job of trying to get even closer to see if he could do something for her, and then actually do it, he shifted as close as he could and then slowly talked to her, trying to keep her calm, while he took a careful look at the injury on her shoulder.

"Hey, girl," he whispered. "That looks mighty uncomfortable. Can I help you with that?"

She just stared at him through the wells of pain in her gaze, and he winced, knowing just how much pain she would be in. He'd been shot a couple times himself—never with an arrow, thank God—but, as he stared at it, he realized that the tip of the arrow was in but wasn't as deep as it could have been.

So, whoever was out there hunting with an arrow was somebody who also didn't know what he was doing. You never left an animal in pain like this, and the newbie hunter probably had no clue how to even operate the equipment he was using. This was a bow and arrow, not a crossbow, and, for that, Timber was grateful because this would be a little bit easier for him to deal with. As he walked closer, the doe stiffened and tried to move.

He froze and whispered, "That won't help. I need you to just stay where you are."

Talking calmly, he felt a hint of a breeze waft through the air. He watched the doe lift her nose and sniff. He did the same, checking for anything out of the ordinary, anything wrong. He noted nothing thankfully. As he stared at the arrow, it was hard for him to still the anger in his heart. That anybody would do this to an animal was just heartbreaking, and to leave her in this condition was even worse. He took another step forward, talking to her.

Just as he got close enough to reach out a hand, she

caught sight of him, or maybe of Kojack at his side. He called Kojack to heel. Kojack stepped back and waited, giving him room. It wasn't the first animal they'd come across that needed help, and it wouldn't be the last one. But Timber could hope that, if he got to her and could help her, she would accept it. She slowly sank down onto her front legs, her back giving out underneath her, as she collapsed, staring up at him. There was hope in her gaze, also fear, but the hope itself was waning.

He finally managed to get close enough to crouch beside her. He took a look at the arrow and realized it had a screw-in head on it, so holding the head firmly against her flesh, he quickly unscrewed the long handle of the wood from the shaft. With that part out, he took a quick glance to see just how bad the injury was. It had penetrated enough that it was excruciating with every step she took, yet it wasn't anywhere near bad enough to kill her.

It had just caused her such pain with every movement that it was more than she could bear. It didn't take him much but one harsh pull to extract it. It didn't have a barb on the end and came out clean. She cried out with the pain, but then her pain was gone. She stared at him, and he wondered if he could run to the house and get his medications and return to find her here. He had to, so that he could clean up the wound and could put in a stitch or two.

He rose slowly to his feet, calling Kojack to his side. He moved swiftly to his house and inside to where he kept his medicine chest. He did an awful lot of rough medicine around this place, but sometimes that's all that was needed. Grabbing his kit, he slowly returned to the doe. As he got to the spot, she was still there. She seemed to be calmer and in a lot less pain and distress. He smiled as he crouched beside her again and quickly cleaned the wound. Then, grabbing the suture material, he stitched the muscle underneath that had been pierced and sliced, then slowly moved his way back out of the wound, until the skin itself was closed. And, with a final application of an ointment to fight infection, he stepped back and smiled at her. He murmured, "Looks as if you might be good to go."

She stared at him but remained quiet, not moving, just resting.

He nodded. "Rest for as long as you need to." And, with that, he stepped back, taking Kojack with him, slowly and steadily putting more distance between them. He hoped that she got the message. When he turned around the next few times, she was still there, just watching him. He smiled and added, "There's no rush. Take your time."

Almost as if she understood and heard him, she stayed quiet for the longest time. When he came out after dinner a little bit later to check on her, she was still there. He frowned, concerned there might be another injury he hadn't seen. Just as he was wondering if he should try to get close to her again, she slowly got up and started to eat the grass around her, and that was the sign that he'd been waiting for.

With that, he smiled and let her just rest and work her way through some food. He had water but none close by. It was on his lists of things to do, to get a water catcher system outside, but he hadn't done that yet. He had one for collecting rain, but he didn't have a trough yet. So he grabbed a bucket, filled it with water from the rain barrel, and moved it closer to her. Then putting it in plain sight, he backed off and let her have access to it, if that's what she needed.

By the time he made it back to his cabin again, he saw

her drinking. He smiled, thinking that, as days went, today had been pretty decent. Now, if only he had an idea who the hell was clumsily hunting deer with a bow and arrow. Considering the fact that he owned all the acreage around here, it bothered him more than a little because this was private property. Not only was no hunting allowed, it was intended to be a refuge for animals, so no hunting of any kind would be tolerated around his place.

Perhaps he needed to go look around and find out who was causing this kind of chaos, although they may well be long gone since he couldn't kill an animal with a shot like that. Either way, it wasn't good for anybody. With the two dogs, Kojack and Philly, loaded up into the back of the truck, he slowly drove out of his place and down around the roads. He stayed to the paved road to see if anything was there. When he didn't see anybody, he moved slowly back toward the property.

He parked the truck, walked over to his pasture, where the deer had come from, and called over his gelding, Sparky. Timber slipped a halter over his chestnut face, buckled it up on the side, and, using a stump, he quickly clambered up onto his back and walked him bareback around the property. He kept an eye out for anything that was off, and there was always something off. It was just a fact of life.

As he moved slowly, he caught sight of something in the distance. He froze, wondering what it was, then moved a little closer and found a tent and several men, sitting around a fire, a case of beer between them as they laughed and chortled. When he came through the trees and stopped just at the edge of their camp, silence fell. He looked at them, his tone calm but dark, as he announced, "You're on private property."

One of the men hopped up and replied, "No, we're on Andy's property, and we've got permission to be here."

"No," Timber stated calmly. "This isn't Andy's property anymore. This is my property. And you are trespassing."

"What the hell?" the one guy asked, glaring at him. "No way. We've been coming here for years."

"Coming here and doing what?" Timber asked, glaring at him. "Hunting?"

"What do you think?"

"Are you the one who left that arrow in the doe?"

The guy frowned at him. "Oh, she survived that?" he asked, then laughed.

Timber continued to glare at him. "Yeah, she survived that, and, as you've admitted yourself, you're hunting on private property."

"What then? You want a percentage of the kill?" he asked, with a mocking look in Timber's direction.

He shook his head. "No, you need to vacate the premises, or I'll be calling the cops."

"Oh, wow, as if we care," replied the head guy, a playfulness in his tone. "Seeing how this isn't even your property."

At that, the other two men started to laugh.

Timber smiled at them and repeated, "You are on private property, and that's not allowed. So, get your asses off my property now …"

"Or what," asked one of the men, with another laugh. "It's not as if you'll stop us."

"Really?" Timber replied. Moving Sparky forward, he came up closer and stated, "This is your final warning. Get the hell off my property now. If I see you here again, and you're using unlawful weapons and hunting anything on these acres, I'll feel free to shoot back."

At that, the men stopped and stared at him. "What the hell?"

Timber's anger built. "You come onto somebody else's posted property, you hunt an animal, and you don't even take care of the fact that you wounded an animal and left her to exist in pain, while you're sitting here drinking beer?"

"We couldn't find her," the main guy shared, without any shame. "We tried to track her, but we couldn't."

"That's because you don't know what the hell you're doing, and, because of your lack of skill, you shouldn't have access to weapons," Timber said, pointing toward the road. "Get your asses off my private property."

"It's not your place. It's Andy's, and we're not going anywhere," snapped the one young man who seemed to be their leader, and he looked pissed.

One of the others got up and added, "Look." He swung an arm toward his buddy. "Obviously he seems to think that this is Andy's place. We haven't been here in a while and just assumed it was still Andy's."

"He would have told us so," said the angry leader of this group.

"No, he wouldn't have," the second guy argued, followed by a snort. "Hell, you didn't even ask the last couple times you came here."

The one who had been talking out of his ass shot him a hard look and snapped, "You shut the fuck up."

"No, I won't," he said, glaring at him. "You told me that it was all cool and that we were allowed here." He turned to face Timber. "Sorry, man, I'm not trying to get in your way."

Timber raised one eyebrow. "Then you're leaving now, right?"

"We could leave in the morning," he suggested a bit sheepishly.

"No," Timber growled. "You're leaving now."

The guy flushed, looked at his two friends, and grimaced. "I don't think they'll go for that."

Timber nodded. "You're leaving now on your own, or I'll confirm that you do."

"Whoa, whoa, whoa, whoa, whoa, what the hell is all this trouble about?" asked the third man, finally speaking for the first time.

"Are you deaf?" Timber asked. "You're on private property. You're hunting without permission, and you're not allowed here. You've already injured one animal and left her to suffer, and now I want you to get the hell off my land."

"*Pfft*. You don't have the means to get us off here," the leader declared arrogantly, standing up and glaring at Timber. "I told you already, … this isn't your fucking land, so I don't care who and what you think you are—"

"Call him," Timber interrupted. "Call Andy and ask him."

The blowhard hesitated. Then his buddies looked at him, and he shrugged. "It's not as if I'll bother him at this hour of the day."

"Meaning that you don't have a clue if it's still his land or not," Timber pointed out, with a nod, "and you're too damn scared to ask him in case it isn't. I'm telling you right now it isn't, and now I'm calling the cops and the game warden." He pulled out his phone and was already texting.

"Whoa, whoa, whoa … What the hell?" asked the second guy, jumping up. "We've been hunting here for years."

"I don't care if you've been hunting here for decades," Timber added, staring at him. "I told you repeatedly to get off my land."

The third man, obviously sensing that things were heading south very quickly, immediately got up and started packing up his gear.

The brash one looked at his buddy, staring him down. "No way. I'm not leaving," he announced, "and no freaking way this guy will make me."

The quieter one hesitated, then explained, "If it's his land, we're in the wrong, and, if we're in the wrong, he's in the right, and that means he can shoot us. You may be good with that, but I am not sticking around to get a load of buckshot up my ass."

"That's a really good point," agreed the second one.

"No, it's not a really good point." The leader sneered. "He doesn't have any right to kick us off. I told you before that this is Andy's land."

The quiet guy just kept packing up all their gear.

The second guy added, "And if you can't show us that Andy still owns it, then I'm not sure I believe you."

The head guy glared at his friends and asked, "What the hell?"

"Yeah. … What the hell?" the second guy repeated. "That's kind of how we feel too. We came here for a hunting trip, and, right about now, I'm not sure what the hell we have."

"What we have is some washed-up guy who thinks he's in the right," the angry young man said, and all of a sudden a rifle was pointed right at Timber.

He stared at the rifle, looked over at the young man holding it, and stated, "And now you've crossed the line. You've got about ten seconds to pull back and to get yourself on the right side of this."

"I'm already right where I should be," the man said, with a sneer. "This is not your place. This is Andy's place, and we are allowed to hunt here." When the bark on a tree just above his head exploded all around him, he lost his footing and slammed to the ground, his friends immediately backing up, their hands in the air.

Timber was a quick-draw expert and always carried a gun stowed in his waistband. He rested it in his lap as he studied them all. "I've warned you enough. Now get the hell off my land."

The other two scrambled over to their friend, who was struggling to his feet. He looked at Timber and declared, "I don't know who you think you are, but believe me that I won't forget this."

Timber nodded. "I've got a cross already made up with your name on it."

"You don't know my name, ... so obviously you don't."

"Yeah, well, *Loser* will do."

And, with that, he moved Sparky back ever so slightly, giving them a little bit of space to pull back and to quickly get their tent down, so they could load up. The other two men didn't say a word. They were quick to pack up, and Timber waited until they were loaded up in their vehicle.

Still in shock, the head guy didn't say a hell of a lot, but it was obvious that he was steaming with a fury that would explode at some point in time. As Timber watched him, he knew he was a rattler in the grass. He knew plenty of men like that, but they weren't men he would allow to come back. "And just in case you didn't get the message, there's no hunting on my land."

"How the hell are we supposed to know which is your land?" he asked cryptically, snarling.

"I'm sure you noticed, as you drove in, that every mile has a sign posted that says No Hunting Allowed on Private Property." Timber smiled at him. "No way you didn't see them."

"We ignored them," the third man admitted. "He told me that they were just there to scare away people who weren't allowed to be here."

The second man, getting into the truck, glared at his angry friend and muttered, "I'll remember that."

The leader flushed, then looked over at his other buddy, the quiet one, who just shook his head at the others. Then he shrugged and added, "This is a bad deal, man. I'm going home."

"What do you mean, you're going home?" the leader asked furiously. "We came here to party, and I came here to hunt," he yelled, spitting fire. "You hear me? ... Yeah, I think we'll hunt. Regardless of whose land he thinks it is." And, with that parting remark, he slammed the truck door and drove off in a harsh cloud of dust, leaving ruts behind.

Timber quickly took note of the license plate, pulled out his phone, and texted it to the game warden and the cops.

If he was lucky, somebody would give a crap enough to chase down these guys and to make an arrest. But Timber highly doubted that anybody would care enough. Most of the people here believed in live and let live, and that worked fine—until it impacted them and their property. But these losers were gone, at least for the moment.

Timber just wasn't sure how long that would last.

Author's Note

Thank you for reading Zander: Hathaway House, Book 26! If you enjoyed the book, please take a moment and leave a short review.

Dear reader,

I love to hear from readers, and you can contact me at my website: www.dalemayer.com or at my Facebook author page. To be informed of new releases and special offers, sign up for my newsletter or follow me on BookBub. And if you are interested in joining Dale Mayer's Reader Group, here is the Facebook sign up page.
http://geni.us/DaleMayerFBGroup

Cheers,
Dale Mayer

About the Author

Dale Mayer is a *USA Today* best-selling author, best known for her SEALs military romances, her Psychic Visions series, and her Lovely Lethal Garden cozy series. Her contemporary romances are raw and full of passion and emotion (Broken But … Mending, Hathaway House series). Her thrillers will keep you guessing (Kate Morgan, By Death series), and her romantic comedies will keep you giggling (*It's a Dog's Life*, a stand-alone novella; and the Broken Protocols series, starring Charming Marvin, the cat).

Dale honors the stories that come to her—and some of them are crazy, break all the rules and cross multiple genres!

To go with her fiction, she also writes nonfiction in many different fields, with books available on résumé writing, companion gardening, and the US mortgage system. All her books are available in print and ebook format.

Connect with Dale Mayer Online

Dale's Website – www.dalemayer.com
Twitter – @DaleMayer
Facebook Page – geni.us/DaleMayerFBFanPage
Facebook Group – geni.us/DaleMayerFBGroup
BookBub – geni.us/DaleMayerBookbub
Instagram – geni.us/DaleMayerInstagram
Goodreads – geni.us/DaleMayerGoodreads
Newsletter – geni.us/DaleNews

www.ingramcontent.com/pod-product-compliance
Lightning Source LLC
Chambersburg PA
CBHW070954180726
48291CB00004B/1288